LOVING THE DOG GROOMER

CINDY ERVIN HUFF

Dedicated to my children, Nicole Arzola Huff, and David Huff. Dog Groomers extraordinaire. Love you guys so much.

1

"Man, you are in so much trouble." Marc Graham tugged the leash of the giant brown matted-haired dog. "Brownie, out of the car." The door to the Puppy Pamper Palace loomed ahead. "Come on." Marc's shoulders slumped. "What is it with you?"

Brownie leaped over the backseat into the back of the SUV, jerking the leash out of Marc's hands.

"Do you have radar or something?" He slammed the back door shut, stepped to the rear of the car, and raised the hatch. Brownie jumped into the back seat again and squeezed over the console into the front seat.

"Fine, be that way." Marc got back in the driver's seat, forcing the huge dog to scramble over the console again. Brownie settled himself on his blanket in the backseat. His lop-sided grin of satisfaction in the rearview mirror added to Marc's irritation.

"Lord, what am I going to do? You led me to this stupid mutt." This was the third time in a week he'd tried to get Brownie to a groomer. "If I had my way." His jaw tightened with frustration. "You'd still be at the pound." He slammed the car door, then clicked his seatbelt.

He wrinkled his nose and glanced back at Brownie, whose innocent eyes didn't acknowledge his contribution to the air pollution. "Really?" Marc gagged and cracked his window. "You just had to get into the garbage at home." The odor of dietary dilemma mixed with the unwashed pooch canceled the car deodorizer. "I could use a little help here." He raised his face heavenward for a moment before starting the car and moving on.

Turning left on Main Street, his eye caught a storefront with a large sign proclaiming Doggie Designer Duo and depicting a dog sitting happily under a hairdryer. Where had he heard of this place? The Sunday paper. Recalling the article's picture of a guy with a mustache and a tattooed forearm posing with a well-groomed poodle brought a chuckle. He'd won some award for grooming.

"Maybe that guy can deal with you." Marc smiled at the canine through the rearview mirror. Brownie sat up and stared out the window.

He parked in front of the shop. "Grammie said don't bring you home without a bath." He turned, making eye contact. "If not for me, do it for her. Do it for Tyler." Would his grandmother turn out his son's therapy dog? Maybe not, but Brownie didn't need to know that. Good grief he was giving the dog more credit for intelligence than the mutt deserved.

Marc opened the back door, sweeping his hand in a downward motion. Brownie came out without a fuss.

"Now you comply." He grabbed the leash, then squatted to get on the dog's level. "Tyler needs you, I get that. You're the only reason he sleeps at night. But I need you to cooperate." Brownie slapped his face with a soggy tongue. Marc grimaced and wiped his cheek. "I hope that's a yes."

He tugged on the leash, and the two headed toward the door.

BRIA WILLIS OPENED the back door of Doggie Designer Duo Salon. She'd spent the morning grooming the newest arrivals at BowWow Rescue. The two Cocker Spaniel mixes had hot spots, infected areas that needed a vet's care, Both dogs had damaged paw pads from neglect. They'd been rescued from a puppy mill where the dogs spent their days in cages.

Making the two more comfortable by bathing and grooming them brought her more joy than any charity event she'd held in her former life. And now that she was President of BowWow Rescue's board, she hoped to make a bigger impact.

Bria noted the hair around a dog grooming station as she passed through the shop. The barks of dogs waiting in crates for their parents echoed in the room. She smiled at her burley brother and partner in the front lobby.

"How's the schedule look, Aaron?" She removed the scrunchie from her ponytail and pulled it tighter, refastening it as she entered the front of the grooming shop.

At the counter, her brother leaned toward the computer screen while standing with the phone to his ear. "Can you bring Bucky in at ten tomorrow?"

His nose wrinkled, and his brows arched as he listened to his client. "Yes, I have the pink dye. He'll look fantastic, I promise."

Bria grinned and shook her head, visualizing Bucky's new do. Shelves full of trophies decorated the wall behind the counter, declaring Aaron a master groomer. She admired his creative talent but found her niche as Doggie Designer Duo's more conservative groomer. Bria picked up the picture of the grand opening of the shop off the top shelf behind the counter. She'd returned to her hometown five years ago, emotionally broken. Her brother had taken her on as his assistant, and now they were equal partners. If not for his loving support, she'd have never survived. Life surrounded by canines who loved and needed her was fulfilling.

Aaron nodded and uh-hummed a few times before he laid the phone in the cradle. "Poor Bucky."

"Mrs. Archer wants her labradoodle pink?" Bria came around the counter and tried to peek over his broad shoulders at the schedule on the screen. She nudged him, and he moved.

"Yeah, something about looking his best for her daughter's princess party." Aaron laughed and scrolled down the screen. "Yep, that was my last appointment. Pick-up for the last three dogs should be within the hour. All I have left is cleaning my station."

"I appreciate having Mondays at the rescue, it revives my spirit to know I'm helping those dogs find a forever home. I'll throw a load of dirty towels in the washer." Bria stretched her back.

"How are things going at the rescue? You know you can always bring the dogs here. We have a better setup."

"It was only two cocker mixes. Poor dogs need a loving home." Bria patted his brother's arm. "This week's schedule is full. What's next week's look like?"

"Monster big." Aaron flexed his shoulders as he stood straighter. "We can handle it. Remember, January slows way down, and we'll be begging for a schedule like this." Aaron patted her arm as the doorbell rang. The distinctive odor of skunk permeated the space as a black standard poodle walked beside his owner, who had a hanky to his nose.

Bria pinched her nose while Aaron waved a hand in front of his face. "Woo wee, Royal, where have you been?"

A middle-aged man signaled for Royal to sit. "His friendliness wasn't well received. My wife said you could fix this." Mr. Wright's mournful expression relaxed with Aaron's thumbs up.

"Sure thing." Aaron took the leash and held it away from his body. "Royal, come on back." He led him to the bathing area as his owner left.

Bria threw the towels in the washer before pulling her high stool up to the counter and clicking on the accounting program. She was behind on balancing the books for last month. The bell rang before she could even look at the spreadsheet.

A tall man entered, attempting to drag a large dog into the room. *Possibly a lab, collie, and... I don't know what. What a tangled mess. This'll be a challenge.* Bria covered her smile as she noticed how the owner's mussy blonde hair fell across his forehead. *Thirtyish, not a gym rat like Aaron. So cute. Stop it, Bria.*

The brown mass stumbled partway inside, then froze. His owner grabbed the dog around its middle and tugged. A whine split the air as the dog planted his feet and sniffed the air.

Bria approached the pair and addressed the dog in a gentle voice. "Hello, fella, look what I have for you?" She held the dog treat near his nose, then stepped back a few feet, and the canine followed. Once inside, she gave him the treat and held her hand out for him to smell. After he sniffed it, she rubbed between his hair-covered eyes.

"How are you doing, boy? You look familiar." Her hands moved under his chin. The speckled-brown dog snuggled close, and his tongue hung out in contentment.

Bria looked up at the owner as she gave the dog a final pat on the head. "How can I help you today?"

"You already have." His eyes held a smile. "Brownie needs a bath and a haircut."

Bria went behind the counter, Brownie followed. "Hey, boy, I need to get your daddy's name." The big dog reclined on the floor at her feet as she found the new client form on the computer.

"Marc Graham, and I'm not his daddy. No way. I doubt he considers me his friend. My son, Tyler, is his owner. They're best buds."

"I'm Bria, I'll need some basic information." She caught him staring at her before he glanced at Brownie. A warmth rather than a shiver spread over her from his gaze. *Let it go, Bria.*

"And what have you done with the monster?" he said. "I have never seen him this calm."

"Well, I'm no dog-whisperer. He may revert to terror once I take him back to groom him." She wiggled the computer's mouse. After gathering the basics from him, she stared at the screen for a moment.

"Claremont Street." Bria glanced up to find his sapphire eyes looking back. Butterflies did aerobics in her stomach. Directing her gaze at the computer again, she said, "I'm your neighbor. My house is up the block from you. Doesn't Delores Carter live there?"

"You know my grandmother?" He pushed stray hairs off his forehead and grinned at her.

"She brought me cookies when I moved in a few years ago. My house used to belong to her best friend. When I'm out running, I stop and talk with her if she's out in the yard tending her flowers. Tyler must be the little red-headed boy I saw walking with her to the ice cream truck last night."

"Yeah, I wish that truck wouldn't come by at all. Sugary treats make him hyper. Too much makes him throw up."

"My mom felt the same way about ice cream trucks. My siblings and I suspect that's why my parents moved to the family farm when my grandparents passed." They shared a grin. Then she typed in his cell number and email. "Now, is he allergic to anything?"

"Have no idea." Marc's embarrassed smile was endearing. She scrolled to the next screen.

"Has he ever been groomed before?"

Marc looked down at his charge. "It's a good possibility. I've tried three other groomers, and he's never gotten past the door. He's a rescue, they shaved him down before we got him."

"I volunteer as a groomer at Bowwow rescue. I love giving them an extra advantage to find a forever home. Did you get Brownie there?" Bria made notes in the comment section, then leaned down and patted Brownie's head. The sweet, trusting look that glimmered in his eyes reminded her of her prize-winning collie, Clarence.

"Maybe, Grammie and Tyler picked him out together. I don't recall where. His hair grew out so thick and tangly in a matter of weeks."

"Let's take him back and see how he does." She opened the half-door separating the front waiting room from the rest of the shop. "Let's go, boy." He stood to follow. She gave a professional smile to Marc. "We give new clients a tour. Helps them feel more comfortable leaving their babies with us."

Marc followed Bria to the grooming area. Brownie stood like a stone. Marc tugged and coaxed until he'd pulled the canine skidding on his paws a few steps. Then Brownie plopped on the floor and refused to move.

"I'm so sorry." Embarrassment colored his neck. He tugged the leash, and the dog stretched his head over his paws and moaned. She held her laugh in check. The poor guy was trying too hard to be in control.

"It's fine." Bria took the leash and nodded. She sat on the floor and petted the giant dog. "Come on, Brownie, you can do this."

"Want to bet?" Marc crossed his arms and scowled at his dog.

"I learned a few tricks from my brother that always calm the most terrified beasts."

A few extra treats didn't hurt.

"I hate to use a muzzle or ask owners to sedate their pets." She stroked Brownie between the eyes. "The extra time loving on them beforehand often works wonders."

She looked up at Marc and caught him staring again. She pointed. "See the tattooed muscle man in the bathing room? That's my brother, Aaron. We own the shop." Usually, the sight of Aaron kept the interested guys at bay. Dating was way off her life radar.

After a few minutes more of Bria's loving attention, Brownie rose and walked beside her. Marc flanked his dog.

Bria stroked Brownie's fur. "I'll take him back to the bathing room. Once he's clean we'll have to shave him down again. Then his nails need clipping. Let's make his first visit positive and simple. Combing out these tangles would be a nightmare for him."

MARC TRIED to keep his mouth from falling open. The confidence in her voice as she chatted with the troublemaker impressed him. The dog stood transfixed, staring up at Bria. Brunette tendrils framed her face as she patted the dog. When Brownie leaped onto her grooming table, Marc shook his head.

Bria fastened the safety collar for the table around his neck. "You're getting ahead of me, boy." She laughed and pressed a button that lowered the table.

"Now that you've test-driven the table, let's get to that bath." She unhooked the safety collar and Brownie came to her side.

"This might take a while." She ran her fingers over the dog, then pointed toward the door. "I'm estimating about three hours. Most people pick their pets up later."

"Three hours?"

"Takes time to make him beautiful." Bria stroked Brownie's head.

"Okay, that'll give me time to get Scooter, I mean Tyler, from school and get a few groceries. Since it's just me and Tyler Brownie has really helped calm him. And he won't want to be away from his friend for very long.." Marc opened the half-door and closed it. From his vantage point, he could take in her tall curvy form and pert nose. When her eyes caught his, he grinned.

Bria frowned for a nanosecond, then gave a bright smile and made a shooing gesture. "Go on. I promise to take good care of him."

Marc nodded and walked out of the grooming shop, his mind fixated on her green eyes. Two blocks away he halted. "Oh, man. My car's back there." He walked nonchalantly back to Doggie Designer Duo and slid into his car. *Hope no one saw that.* He stared at the sign before backing out of his space. *She's beautiful and a dog lover.*

Marc shook his head. Beautiful on the outside didn't mean beautiful on the inside. His late wife's image haunted him as he pulled out of the parking space. Her looks had drawn him in and ruined his life. Marc glanced at the dash clock and headed to Tyler's school.

Brownie's presence helped his son cope and rest at night. But the mongrel's misbehavior added to Marc's anxiety. *Maybe Bria'll be the one to tame that monster.* He smiled as he pulled up in front of Tyler's school.

2

Marc adjusted his son's car seat. Then he took out his comb and attempted to wrestle the boy's cowlick into submission.

"Stop it, Daddy." Tyler's green eyes warned of a tantrum. He glanced around the car. "Where's Brownie?"

"Getting a haircut." Marc kept his voice light.

"I need Brownie." His voice rose an octave and his hands fisted.

"Scooter, after we get a few things at the store, we'll go pick up Brownie."

"I want to pick him up now." Tyler scowled and kicked the back of the front seat.

Marc placed his hand on his son's leg to stop the motion.

"If you can be patient, we'll get star cookies at the store."

Tyler's face squished into a thoughtful frown. "Can I have two boxes?"

"Sure." Marc hated bribery, but his son's panic attacks and hyperventilating broke his heart. Janice's death had brought on more anxiety.

"You promise we get to pick up Brownie right after."

"Yes—no. We need to get the groceries to Grammie before we pick up Brownie."

"Why?"

"What happened the last time Brownie was in the car with the groceries?"

"He ate steak." Tyler giggled, placing his hand over his mouth, a sparkle in his eyes.

Marc wanted to avoid the last fiasco. He'd opted to go to the park and then the grocery store for a few things for dinner last Monday. Visions of destroyed grocery bags, and Brownie's satisfied smirk as he gulped down the last steak, fortified his resolve to get Brownie later. Oh, why'd he let the counselor talk him into a dog?

Marc started the SUV.

"We should get him doggie treats 'cause he's scared."

"You know, Scooter, he's not scared. He likes the lady."

"Really? She must be something special 'cause Brownie don't like everybody."

"She must be." Marc wondered what she'd think of Tyler as he pulled into the store parking lot. His son chattered the whole time they shopped. "Look, Daddy, a Spiderman cup. That's so cool." He reached for it.

Marc placed his son's hands on the cart. "Help me, please."

The therapist had stressed redirection rather than scolding.

Marc placed cookies in the cart. "Thank you, Daddy." Tyler smiled and set his focus back on maneuvering the cart around the store.

Twenty minutes later, Marc sighed, reveling in the normalcy of the shopping trip as they exited the grocery store. Now to get the stuff home without an incident. Tyler helped load the groceries into the back of the car. Then he began fidgeting while Marc buckled him into his seat. *There went normal.*

Five minutes later, the quiet in the car was interrupted

"Can we get Brownie now?" Tyler asked through chocolate-covered lips. His left hand gripped the half-eaten candy bar while he drew pictures of Brownie on the window with the chocolate-coated fingers of his right hand.

"You promised me you wouldn't make a mess in the car." Marc glared through the rearview mirror at Tyler. "Remember, we have to take the groceries home. Then you need to wash your face and hands." *And I'll need to clean the window. Why do I give him candy in the car?* Because I'm desperate to keep him quiet.

The counselor had emphasized distracting Tyler in the car because of the accident that had created his trauma. Marc kicked himself for leaving the soothing bag containing small toys and his tablet at home. Chocolate art had been Tyler's favorite behavior when he was three. The pouty, angry face in the rearview mirror signaled a tantrum was eminent. *Please don't digress.* The therapist said Tyler was doing well, but when he made that face, it wrenched Marc's soul. Two long, cleansing breaths stilled his racing heart. *Father, help me redirect Tyler.*

"I want to get Brownie." The seat kicking began.

"I guess you'll have to wait at home." Marc tried to sound confident.

The kicking stopped and his whining began. "Why?"

"Only well-behaved boys are allowed in the dog barbershop."

"Sorry." Tyler pouted. "I miss Brownie."

"Be patient, son."

The turn to their home came into view. Marc's grandmother strolled to the garage, door opener in hand. At seventy, she showed no signs of slowing down. She wore jeans and a stylish blouse, her blond hair streaked with gray. Her invitation to move in had been an answer to prayer. She needed help with her home upkeep after his grandfather passed, and he needed someone to help with Tyler.

Marc grabbed the wipes from a pocket on the door and wrestled the squirming Tyler to clean his hands and face.

"Stop it, I can do it myself." His son grabbed the wipes packet and pushed Marc's hand away. "I'm not a baby."

"You'll need to wash up in the house." Marc unfastened the seatbelt, giving Tyler another moment to calm. "Now, grab a bag."

Marc opened the hatchback and Grammie peeked in a few bags.

"Did you remember my TV Guide?"

"Yes, ma'am. Wouldn't want you to miss NCIS or Jeopardy."

"Don't make fun, now." She whacked him playfully on the wrist with the magazine. "I hate scrolling on that TV guide channel. A quick look inside these pages and done. Besides, I like to read the celebrity stories."

Together, they hauled the groceries to the kitchen. Grammie organized the bags' contents on the table. Marc set the milk in the fridge.

"I got star cookies, Grammie." Tyler plopped his sack on the counter.

While Grammie instructed Tyler how to put the groceries away, Marc pulled out his cell phone and dialed the groomer. "Bria, this is Marc Graham. Is Brownie ready?" He glanced over at his son. "Brownie's ready." Tyler did a fist bump in the air.

"What was that? "Marc returned to his phone call. "A hot spot? You can show me what you're talking about when we get there." Marc ended the call. Tyler, the spitting image of Marc's late wife, put cans on a low shelf in the pantry. Tyler disliked haircuts, and his son's cowlick stood up more noticeably with his hair grown longer. *Maybe seeing Brownie's new haircut will inspire him.*

"Tyler, go to the bathroom, and then we'll go get Brownie."

"I don't need to." Tyler grabbed for the bag of cookies. Marc snatched them from him, placing them on a shelf in the upper cabinet. Tyler scowled and pushed a chair over to get the cookies off the shelf.

"Tyler, we need to go."

"I want cookies first." Tyler climbed onto the chair.

"Go to the bathroom." Marc matched his scowl.

"No." Tyler stretched his hands toward the cookies.

Marc ran his fingers through his hair. "I said go to the bathroom." His son's crinkled pout and squinting eyes meant he was debating his response.

Tyler crossed his arms, jumped off the chair, then kicked it over, glaring at his father.

"Tyler Jonathan, when your father tells you to do something, you best do it." Grammie's stern tone got her great-grandson's attention. He gave a soulful sigh and a solemn nod, then marched off to the bathroom.

"Grams, how do you do it?" Frustration rested in Marc's stomach.

"I raised six children and then you and your sister." Grammie chuckled. "Tyler knows he can't bully me into doing his will."

"He's not bullying." Marc shook his head and stared at his feet for a moment before adding, "He's a traumatized boy."

"I know he was in the car when his mother died, but that doesn't give him the right to carry on until he gets his way. The therapist said he needs boundaries."

"And understanding."

"I don't believe he said spoil and let him have his way."

When small footsteps pounded up the hall, Marc said no more. Grammie was old-fashioned in her child-raising techniques. Overall, he'd learned a lot from her. But he drew the line at paddling. His late wife, Janet, physically abused Tyler when she drank too much, and that was often. He swore to never lay a hand on his boy. Other forms of discipline proved just as challenging when Scooter cried and carried on. He knew he was too softhearted. But somehow, he had to erase the damage he had caused by putting his job before his son.

~

TYLER RACED from the car to the grooming shop.

"Slow down," Marc hollered.

Tyler pranced at the door. "Hurry, Daddy."

Marc grabbed his son's hand and they entered. Brownie's bark caught Tyler's attention.

"I hear him." Tyler stood on his tiptoes and peeked over the half-door. "Why is Brownie in a cage?" Tyler scowled and jerked his hand from Marc. Bria came around the counter. The sweet smile she gave his son warmed his heart. Marc's pulse sped up as she neared. He fidgeted with the change in his pocket and focused on Tyler.

"Hello, I'm Bria." She offered Tyler her hand. Rather than hide behind Marc's leg, his son reached for her hand and shook it.

"I'm Tyler. I'm five years old and in Mrs. Miller's kindergarten class."

Brownie's incessant barking distracted Tyler. He pointed. "Why is Brownie in a cage?"

"When the dogs aren't getting haircuts, we keep them in crates to keep them safe. Come on back."

Bria nodded to Marc to follow and led the way.

"See Royal there?" She pointed at a black poodle in a crate.

"Yes." Tyler stared at the dog.

"He is afraid of other dogs and might bite. Brownie is in a new place, he's calmer in a crate. Some dogs need to be around people, or they get scared. We fasten their leashes on the hooks you see around the room. Then they can watch us and feel safe."

"When can he come out?"

"Soon. Now, he's been telling me all about you."

"He has? Daddy, did you hear that? Bria can understand Brownie." A big smile filled Tyler's face as he looked at her with admiration.

Marc laughed at his son's joy. Such a change from the anger and sadness.

"Dogs always talk about their special people." Bria ruffled Tyler's hair.

"Can you teach me his language?" Tyler neared the crate. Marc placed his hand on his son's shoulder to keep him still.

Brownie whimpered and wiggled.

"See, he's saying you're here at last," said Bria.

"Wow, he got a big haircut." Tyler grinned. The dog looked about twenty pounds lighter now that he was shaved down.

Bria touched Tyler's arm. "Yes, he's more comfortable now. Stand back while I get Brownie out of the crate. You might get hurt if you stand too close when the door opens."

Before Marc could add an exhortation, Tyler stepped away, watching her every move. Bria clicked Brownie's leash to his collar and then whispered in his ear. Then she stepped back and signaled. "Come."

Brownie came toward her. She signaled twice more. "Sit. Stay."

Brownie plopped his backside down and focused on her face. Marc shook his head in amazement. Tyler giggled.

"Show me how." Tyler reached a hand toward Brownie.

Bria took Brownie through a series of hand signals, which he obeyed instantly. *Where have you been all my life?* Marc's attention moved from Bria's actions to Tyler's awed expression. She'd managed in a few minutes to bring out the happy side of his son. An angel of hope with thick brown hair, emerald eyes, and a perfect form.

"Okay, Tyler," she pulled a treat from her pocket, "give him a treat."

"Good dog." Then he gave Brownie a big hug. "You are so smart."

Marc scratched the back of his neck. "How?"

"When Aaron used hand signals with Royal, I noticed Brownie responded. Whoever turned him into the dog rescue had taken time to train him."

"I've never had a dog and didn't know they could be trained like that. My uncle yelled at his dogs when he got frustrated."

"Aaron is a certified dog trainer. I'm sure he'd be happy to work with you two, I mean the three of you."

"Are you certified?"

"Yes." Bria frowned and straightened her back then headed to the counter.

Even her frown intrigued him. The icy glare that melted into a fake smile wasn't lost on Marc. "Can you sign us up for your class?"

"Hey, Aaron." She called to her brother to the front counter. He emerged with a stack of folded towels. "Do you have time in your training schedule for one more?"

Aaron set the towels on the counter. "Sure."

His right arm bore a tattoo of long shears shaped like a dog's muzzle and his other arm sported a cross. Marc cringed at the sight. Janet had gotten three tats. She'd always nagged him to get one. No way would he submit to a myriad of needle sticks, no matter how many times she called him a "coward." Janet accused him of being out of touch with the world.

She'd told him being raised by his grandparents made him act like an old man. Was that such a bad thing? Not after all Tyler went through with her.

Aaron grabbed a business card. "Call me. You don't need a group obedience class because Brownie knows the rules. I just need to teach you."

Marc took one look as his wrestler's build and wasn't about to say he'd prefer Bria as a trainer.

"If Brownie can be obedient, my life will be one-hundred-percent easier."

"Yeah, it's the humans who need training to make life easy." Aaron chuckled. "Excuse me, I need to take Royal to the backyard before his owners come or I'll be mopping the floor again."

Bria squatted beside Brownie. "I wanted to show you something." She ran her hands through his fur and parted it. "Right here."

Marc and Tyler leaned in.

"See that red patch? It's a hot spot. It's a bacterial infection caused by not grooming a dog regularly. Have you noticed him scratching?"

"Yeah, but we didn't see anything." Marc didn't want to admit he avoided touching the mongrel. If Tyler didn't need him, well.... "Does it hurt?"

"The more he scratches it, yes. Hot spots can spread the infection. You need to brush him every day even if he doesn't like it. A vet can give you a prescription to heal the spot. I imagine Brownie's irritable and antsy."

Marc felt dumber than dumb that he hadn't noticed the rash. If he'd combed Brownie every day, then.... "Do you know a good vet?" Another single parent fail.

"I'll give you Dr. Michael's card. He'll clear it right up."

Marc took the card and Brownie's leash. A heaviness sat on his heart. One more failure. One more thing someone else must help him with. Were all single fathers as clueless?

BRIA SWEPT the grooming room one last time, a mindless task that let her imagination wander to the new client and his cute son. She put the broom away as Aaron brought out the mop and a large bucket. He made quick work of mopping the room.

"Why'd you pawn Brownie's dad off on me?"

She went to the reception area and dusted the counter.

Aaron stared at her from the doorway, his elbow resting on the mop handle.

"Don't start." Bria opened the register and counted the day's receipts.

"Seems like a nice guy. Single dad with no clue about dogs. A little one-on-one training could prove interesting." Aaron waggled his eyebrows, then wrung out the mop.

"Seeming nice means nothing." Bria sighed as she recounted the twenties. "He may be nice, and his son's adorable. But...."

"Can't learn to trust if you don't start meeting guys again?"

"Guys like Mitchell?"

"Not every guy is a sleezeball in a designer suit."

When she was at her lowest point—after her twin sister Brittany died of cancer—Mitchell Price had swept in all charm and seduction. He'd propelled her to a new life as a successful model while stealing her self-worth.

"I know. But my guy radar is busted. I'd like to be wanted for more than my looks. Someone who understands me."

"God might just have dumped him on your doorstep."

"You gonna stand there leaning on that mop?"

"Nope." He saluted. The teasing sparkle in his eyes relaxed her.

Aaron disappeared with the mop and returned just as she balanced the receipts. He straightened the merchandise shelves, then checked his phone.

"Hey, sis, I gotta go. Fantasy Football and wings tonight at the Sport's Spot with my bros."

"I'll close up."

"You're the best." Aaron kissed her cheek.

Bria always cringed at her brother's praise. Brittany had been the best, sweet and kind and not shy about her faith. Popular in high school too. The polar opposite of Bria. Brittany's death had torn her in half. The best part of Bria died with her sister, leaving the part that made bad choices behind. Her family's non-judgment policy made coming home easy. Aaron's offer of a job kept her grounded. Vacuuming the reception area, she pushed the memories of the worst three years of her life out of her mind. Once the shop was in order, she locked up and headed to her car.

On the ride home, she tuned in her favorite radio station and cranked up the praise music. The lyrics glided her heart to prayer. *Father, thank You I'm not the girl I was eight years ago when You took Brittany home. Thank You for Aaron and for rescuing me from the lie I was living.* She tapped the steering wheel in time to the music as the streetlights switched on to illuminate the dusky sky. She turned on to her street and pulled into the driveway, then slammed on the brakes.

Brownie stood in her headlights. Tyler darted to the dog's side, grabbed his leash, and tugged.

Bria turned off her car, got out, and signaled to Brownie. He sat beside Tyler.

"Sweetie, what are you doing out at night?"

"Brownie kept bothering Daddy to go out. He was busy, so I took him."

"Don't take Brownie out until you've learned how to make him mind. I'll walk you both home."

A harried Marc jogged up the street. He wore sweatpants, and his pallor matched his white t-shirt. "There you are."

"Brownie found my house, and Tyler found Brownie." Bria tried not to laugh at Marc's fuzzy slippers.

"She's gonna teach me how to make Brownie mind."

"Don't you think a five-year-old is a little young to be walking a dog at night?" Bria placed a protective arm around Tyler.

"He snuck out of the house with Brownie." Marc glowered at the dog. "I guess I can't put that fence off any longer." He knelt in front of his son. "Never take Brownie out by yourself. Do you understand?" He cupped the boy's chin and forced him to look him in the eyes. "Do you understand?"

Tyler's lip quivered. "Yes, Daddy."

Marc hugged his son. "If anything ever happened to you...."

Bria's eyes stung with unushered tears at seeing the love this man had for his son. Jealousy bit at her heart as a tiny face appeared in her thoughts, reminding her of what she'd lost.

Marc looked up at her as he stood. "Sorry, thanks for helping."

"I understand." Bria patted the boy's shoulder, composing herself. "Tyler, be more careful. Brownie is a big dog."

"Yes, ma'am." He hugged her tight. "I'll do better when you teach me." A pinch pricked her heart at the thought of teaching a child.

Marc took Tyler's hand, and the three headed home. Loneliness grabbed her heart as she watched the departing forms enter their home a few blocks away. *Father, will I ever feel safe enough to open my heart and find happiness like that?*

3

B ria pushed the start button on the one-cup coffeemaker. A yawn interrupted her extracting of the English muffin from the bag. She blinked hard, split the muffin, and put it in the toaster while struggling to defog her brain.

Dreams are such stupid things. She padded barefoot to the fridge to get the jam, recalling her teenage-hood dream of marrying the actor, Chris Pratt. *Stupid for sure.*

Thoughts of a certain single dad and his adorable son took center stage. Last night, with every turn and pillow fluff, she'd compared Mitchell with Marc. Mitchell appeared kind, even gallant at first. He'd showered her with gifts and praise. *"You're the most amazing woman. The sky's the limit for you, babe."*

Once she'd signed the modeling contract, the nightmare began. Mitchell stole her self-esteem and her virtue. Faith took a nose-dive into a bucket of shame along the way. Even though Marc and Mitchell appeared as different as salt and pepper, her fatigue-induced dreams last night morphed the kind father into the arrogant businessman.

"Alexis," she spoke to the cylinder on the counter, "play classical mix." Soft music filled the kitchen, pushing away the angst.

A scratch sounded on the front door, once, twice, and then a woof. Brownie's lopsided grin greeted her when she opened the door.

"Really boy?" She stroked his head. "We have to stop meeting like this."

Brownie nuzzled close, then, like a cat, threaded between her legs and almost tripped her. "You're one odd dog." Bria knelt, rubbing his collarless neck. She stared into dark brown doggie eyes. "If you're looking for a girlfriend, I'm not in the market for a relationship."

Bria grabbed Clarence's old leash and collar hanging from the hook beside the door and secured them to Brownie. Fastening it around the mixed breed brought back memories of her sweet collie. Replacing Clarence seemed traitorous. She sighed. Life remained too busy, and it hurt too much when a friend died. Bria rubbed Brownie's silky head. The canine pressed against her hand his signature silly grin focused on her. She leaned in, enjoying the interaction.

"Is Houdini your hero?" Laughing, she rose and gestured for him to heel.

She slipped into a pair of flip-flops.

"Come on, you vagabond. It's time to go back home."

Brownie walked by her side. The cool autumn breeze spread goosebumps on her arms.

Delores Carter's pink, late-model Grand Marquis sat in the driveway of the blue and beige Victorian home. Butterfly stomach began. *Stop. You've visited Delores many times* Indicating for Brownie to sit, she rang the doorbell.

Tyler opened the door dressed in Superman pajamas. Fresh tears glistened on his cheeks. The boy's delightful squeal pushed away all nervousness.

"You found him." Tyler hugged Brownie and smiled up at Bria. "I told Daddy to call you."

"Scooter, what did I say about opening the door?" Marc joined his son, wearing matching Superman pajamas. Bria smothered a giggle.

"Grammie's idea." A blush covered his neck. "Tyler's pjs have a cape."

"Daddy, Brownie likes Bria."

"I see that." Marc stroked his bedhead and smiled. "Apparently, Brownie wants *you* to be his trainer."

Marc's shy smile caught her off-guard. *Nip this thing, whatever it is, in the bud.* Bria searched for her professionalism, hiding beneath this unwanted attraction.

"We stake him out back a few times a day. He figured out how to escape." Marc grabbed Brownie's collar off the counter, squatted before the dog, exchanged collars, and stood. "I told Grammie I'd pay for a fence."

Bria grasped Clarence's old collar and leash, gathering courage from his memory. Clarence had been a proper show dog while on stage—garnering lots of blue ribbons—but fun-loving like Brownie when the spotlights were off. The collie had worn out several Frisbees. At least, the ones she hadn't managed to toss on the roof in their games of fetch.

The spotlight was on her now.

"A fence is a good investment. Dogs don't do well staked outside." *Okay, you can do this. Step out of your comfort zone.* Bria stood with Brownie as a barrier between them. "There's room in my schedule on Tuesday night."

"Tuesday night?"

"To train you and Tyler on how to work with Brownie." *Who am I kidding? I haven't done any dog training since Clarence died.*

"Yeah, right, Tuesday night." Marc stepped toward Brownie and did a hop-wince. Pain flashed across his face. "Ahhhh." Marc stared angrily and spoke through gritted teeth. "Tyler, what have I told you about putting away your Legos?"

Tyler's eyes widened. He froze, then bent to retrieve the offending piece and placed it in the bin on the coffee table.

"Sorry, Daddy." Tyler's eyes glistened. Bria resisted the urge to comfort the boy.

Marc hugged his son and kissed his head. "Good boy. Brownie could have swallowed that."

"Really?" Tyler's expression of concern warmed Bria, as did Marc's sweet response to his son's blunder. The boy reached for Brownie. "I promise to be more careful." The dog nuzzled close to his friend and wagged his tail. Bria couldn't help envying the child for his loving, furry companion.

"What's all the yelping?" Delores emerged from the kitchen door wearing blue workout gear. "Hello, Bria. I see you found Brownie."

"Brownie found me. Good morning, Delores."

"Tyler, you worried for nothing. He always comes back. Today he brought a friend." Delores smiled and winked. "Care to join us for breakfast?" She took Bria's hand in hers.

The smell of blueberries and bacon tempted Bria to stay. If it was only Delores... "Thank you, but no. Today is a full work schedule."

"Don't be a stranger. The neighborhood is always changing, and I have enough strangers in my life." Delores squeezed her hand. "Let's have coffee sometime soon." They exchanged a hug before the older woman went back into the kitchen.

Bria turned to Marc. "Your grandmother and I plan time for coffee a few times a year." She smiled. "She's so sweet to greet the new neighbors on the whole street. They aren't as friendly as when I was a child."

"You grew up around here?" Marc wracked his brain for any memory of a brunette neighbor girl as he peeked around the corner to check Tyler's whereabouts. His son had busied himself forming a Lego tower on the coffee table.

"No, just visited my Aunt Gwen. I bought the house when she passed. She and Delores were good friends."

"I remember. She was...." Marc smirked.

"An old crab." Bria laughed. "Even though Aunt Gwen was anti-social, I have wonderful memories of our time together. My sister and I loved spending the night." Bria glanced at her Smartwatch. "Gotta go, first appointment is in thirty minutes."

Walking toward home the sense of peace Marc brought her dissolved. Having a client living so close was awkward, especially an attractive one. *Stop! Not having a man in my life beyond helping with their dog*

∿

MARC CLOSED the door and groaned as he noticed his pajamas. *Great impression, dude.* "Hey, Scooter, smells like Grammie has breakfast ready."

"Yay!" Tyler leapt up, scattering Legos. "Sorry."

Marc helped him put them away. Tyler took his hand as they headed to the kitchen, Brownie at their heels.

"I like Bria. Brownie likes Bria. I think you should marry her."

Tyler's matter-of-fact statement startled Marc. Did he want to be married again? Maybe someday. But Bria was out of his league. She had her own business, home, and appeared to have it all together. And here he was. Janet's irrational spending and legal fees had forced him to sell everything. *What grown man of any worth lives with his grandmother?*

"In your dreams." Marc nudged Tyler in response to his son's matchmaking comment.

Tyler grinned as Marc sat on a chair at the kitchen island. "If she's in my dreams, you'll marry her? Cool."

"Never mind. Let's eat." Marc grabbed his orange juice and sat beside his son as Grammie set a serving of scrambled eggs on each plate. Marc added a spoonful of mixed fruit on Tyler's plate.

"Strawberries are yucky." Tyler poked at the fruit.

"Then eat the bananas and raspberries."

Grammie set out a basket of blueberry muffins, which brought a smile to Tyler's face. He pushed his plate away and lunged for a muffin. Grammie grabbed the basket and put it on the counter. "Finish what's on your plate first."

"No strawberries." Tyler repeated his instruction and crossed his arms.

"Eat the other fruit and leave the strawberries." Marc glared, what he hoped was the no-nonsense look Grandpa used to give him.

Tyler scowled before picking up a fork and separating the strawberries from the other fruit.

"Encouraging obedience is hard work." Marc started on his eggs while watching Tyler.

"You're coming along." Grammie placed the dirty cooking utensils in the sink, turned, and leaned against the counter. "Janet was an enabler, but you can learn to be a teacher."

"What's an enabler?" Tyler showed his plate to Grammie. Only the strawberries remained. She brought the basket back to the counter, sat beside Tyler, and handed him a muffin.

"An enabler is someone who makes it easy to get away with bad behavior—like when you don't make Brownie obey." Grammie kissed Tyler's head.

"Miss Bria will teach us how to make Brownie obey." Marc snagged a muffin as he rose from his place.

Tyler shoved the last of his muffin into his mouth, crumbs sticking to his chin. "I can't wait to be in Miss Bria's class."

Me too. Marc pointed to the napkins in the holder, and Tyler grabbed one and wiped his mouth. Marc leaned on the counter and finished his muffin while the coffee brewed. He poured a cup as Tyler scurried from the room.

"Hurry so you're not late for school." Marc took two cups of coffee to the table and sat near Grammie, listening for water from the bathroom sink before he spoke.

"Let's not talk about Janet when Tyler's around."

Grammie stirred sugar into her cup. "I don't think Tyler knows his mother's first name. You didn't when you were five."

"He's an insightful kid. If he does remember Janet, I hope they're happy memories."

"He mentioned he enjoys reading while sitting in my lap because he did it with Mommy.

"That's good to know." Marc sighed.

"Stop beating yourself up for what she did. You have the rest of his life to make him feel loved, and you're doing a great job." Grammie kissed his forehead. "Over time, he'll forget the bad memories."

"I hope you're right." Marc left his unfinished coffee and headed to the shower. The warm, steamy water soothed the bitter memories. Janet had loved Tyler very much—when she wasn't drunk.

Marc fell hard for Janet over college spring break, and they married on a whim in their last semester at the University of Illinois. Janet's party-girl persona had captivated him. She was fascinating, flirty, and beautiful. After starting their careers, parties were their weekend activity. But her need to party didn't stop after Tyler was born. Janet's drinking got worse, bringing on a meanness that Marc avoided by working long hours.

He finished getting ready for the day. The consequences of his choices laid heavy on his heart. He stumbled over Brownie, who sprawled on the floor at the bottom of the stairs. The dog yelped.

"Sorry."

Grammie was fussing over re-buttoning Tyler's shirt when Marc entered the living room. *Will I ever be able to undo the abuse Janet meted out while I neglected my son to build my career? No, to avoid confrontations with her. How selfish was that.* "Scooter, we need to go."

He helped Tyler into his backpack. "Today's mission at school?"

"Mind the teacher, learn stuff, and be kind." Tyler ticked them off on his fingers.

"Excellent." Marc kissed his cheek. "You can do this."

"Yes, I can." Tyler nodded.

Marc hugged him extra tight before grabbing the car keys.

4

Bria checked her makeup in the bathroom mirror. She'd rushed home from work and dashed into the shower. Usually, Tuesdays held a light schedule. Plenty of time to get home before the seven o'clock class with the Grahams. Today Aaron added two bath dogs to her schedule and an emergency de-skunking, pushing her three o'clock end-time to five o'clock. A quick stop at Panera for a bite, and the clock read six.

"Why?" Bria frowned at her reflection. "Makeup?"

She'd kept the colors subtle and natural. Temptation to wash it off gnawed at her. This wasn't a date. "It's all Aaron's fault." Bria sighed and brushed her shoulder-length hair. "He put the thought in my mind." Dark curls hung in thick waves. A tug upward and a new hair tie produced a serviceable ponytail. "Better."

"We Are the Champions" ringtone vibrated her phone as Bria headed toward the front door. "Hey, Aaron."

Loud music in the background soon softened. "Do you need me to take your class?"

"No."

"I was a jerk for teasing you." Aaron had turned off the music.

"It's fine. Brownie is my newest stalker. A dog treat or a pat on the head keeps him happy." *If only the paparazzi had been so easily dissuaded.*

"Okay, then." Aaron's worry phrase. "If you need rescuing, call."

"My hero." Bria laughed. "No worries. Between Tyler, Delores Carter, and not to mention Brownie, I'll be safe. Love you, bye."

Aaron had taken the job as protector to guard-dog level since Mitch. Bria knew the time to move forward had come. Not all men were Mitchell. At least that was the mantra playing in her mind, but her heart muted its beat. How many men were kind all the time, not just first dates? Tonight wasn't a date, but taking directions from a woman crossed into a test of character. Would she discover Marc placed in the same class of good men as Dad? Or was he all show-dog fluff?

~

MARC OPENED THE DOOR, and Tyler exchanged a warm hug with Bria. "Right on time."

Bria's teal blouse hung past the waistband of her jeans. Pink toenails peeked out of white sneaker sandals. The living room lighting reflected in her green eyes, enhancing her smile.

Marc's knot of nervousness tightened when a bird tattoo flitted across his vision. It stretched from her left wrist to her elbow. How had he not seen it before? Janet had loved her menagerie of tattoos.

Did Bria have more? It was unfair to compare Bria to his late wife, but the checklist formed anyway. Janet's tats had been her way of rebelling against settling into married life. It represented her too-free spirit. Bria didn't seem the type.

"Where's Brownie?" Bria looked around.

"In the backyard." Marc forced the comparison from his mind and closed the front door. "They finished the fence today. Brownie's been eager to be outside."

"I'll get him, Miss Bria." Tyler ran toward the kitchen.

"Miss Bria?" She pushed a stray hair out of her face and chuckled.

Marc's nervousness abated with the melodic sound. "Grammie frowns on children addressing adults by their first names."

"How Southern."

"You got that right. Grammie grew up in Tennessee, met my grandfather at Moody Bible Institute in Chicago, and never left Illinois."

"I thought Mr. Carter was a banker."

"Grandpa was a financial planner. But he went to Moody for Bible classes. Grammie was studying children's ministry."

"My aunt mentioned something about her running children's church.

Aunt Gwen considered church for children foolishness. The church she attended bored my sister and I to death. A little foolishness would have been nice." Bria laughed and added, "It's Willis."

It took Marc a moment to realize she was telling him her last name.

"But Tyler may call me Miss Bria." Her smile brought attention to her full lips, causing his neck to warm. Marc diverted his gaze to his stocking feet. Still standing, he grabbed a pair of sneakers near the couch and maneuvered his feet inside. The heel of the left shoe curled. He plopped on the sofa, feeling like a high school boy in gym class. Each tug of the shoestrings served as a reminder to rein in his growing attraction. A repeat of the past was not happening.

"Shall we do the class outside or in here?" he asked. He'd paid extra to get the fence installed before the classes started. The furry nuisance would have nowhere to hide in the enclosed yard.

"Daddy, come here." Tyler's voice quavered.

They ran to the back door.

"Brownie is gone." Tyler tugged his dad's hand.

A fresh hole rested under the fence. Marc groaned, and Bria giggled.

"You think this is funny?" His awkwardness forgotten as memories of Janet laughing at crises took its place. His jaw flexed. "There is nothing funny about my escaped felon."

"I'm sorry." Bria's eyes still held glee. "Dogs that aren't used to fences sometimes do this. Let's search for him."

Tyler raced ahead and struggled to open the gate. Marc reached his son and unlatched it. Tyler darted out onto the sidewalk, following the sound of barking. A car sped by as Marc dashed to keep up, his heart beating a dirge of fear.

"Wait up." Marc's tone got the wanted response.

Tyler stopped in the center of the sidewalk. "Brownie's chasing a squirrel." Tyler waved as he bounced on his heels for Marc to hurry. The dog paused a block ahead as the squirrel flitted up a tree.

By the time they'd all caught up, Brownie rested his paws against the tree, barking and whining as his tail lashed. The squirrel sat on a high branch, out of range and issuing chittering taunts.

"Brownie." Tyler and Marc called in unison. The dog ignored them.

"Come." Bria's voice rang firm. Brownie stopped barking and stared their way.

"Come."

The canine ran to her side.

Marc stared, sure his mouth hung to his chest.

"Wow, Miss Bria. He likes you best." Tyler's awe was evident.

Bria signaled for Brownie to sit. "No, my voice was commanding. You two were scared mommas."

"Should I run and get his leash?" Marc scowled at the smiling mutt.

"Let me try something first." Bria patted the dog's head. "Brownie." They made eye contact. "Heel." He obeyed and walked at her hip.

Marc and Tyler followed them up the sidewalk. Her ability to control the furry menace impressed Marc. He made a note on the pro-side of his mental list of why she was worth getting to know better. Tyler ran ahead and opened the gate. Brownie stopped and planted his feet. Marc crossed his arms and waited to see how she handled his stubborn stance.

Bria kneeled beside him and held his massive head in her small hands. "It's all right, boy, you can do this." Another hand signal and Brownie walked into the fenced-in yard. "Good boy."

Marc shook his head with a chuckle. After they'd all stepped through, Tyler fastened the gate.

"Bring his leash." Bria leaned down and petted Brownie. "We need to get him use to the fence."

Marc brought the leash. Bria walked Brownie around the yard, tugging the leash every time he neared the fence issuing a commanding "No." When they reached the hole he'd dug, she scowled. "Bad dog." Brownie's head sagged.

Bria turned her attention to them. "Someone needs to be with Brownie in the yard for at least a few days. When he goes near the fence, say no and call him to you. Every time he does his business in a designated corner say, 'good dog.'"

"You can train a dog to do that?" Marc scratched his head.

"If you want to limit his toilet area, yes."

She directed the next instruction at Tyler. "Be sure to have poop bags to keep the yard clean. Pick it up every time he goes to avoid a massive mine field and poo on shoes."

Tyler nodded. Marc grinned, pleased at how serious the boy was about caring for Brownie.

"Play with him in the fenced-in yard." Bria continued her instructions. "Make this a friendly place." Turning to Marc, "Try not to make it a place of punishment, or where you send him when company comes."

Had she read his mind? Brownie was overly friendly with visitors and, to Marc's chagrin, had figured out how to open the laundry room door.

"Before we are done with our classes, you'll all be trained in company etiquette and obedience." Bria patted Brownie's head and ruffled Tyler's hair.

For the next hour, Bria coached the basics. Marc's anxiety faded as the dog followed his commands. When his hand position was wrong, Brownie stared and cocked his head. Bria laughed and adjusted Marc's fingers. Heat surged his arm. When Marc messed up again, her closeness and sweet smile intensified the urge to kiss her. Instead, he moved away from the source of the inappropriate thought and gathered his wits. Apparently, he'd forgotten how to remain professional around the opposite sex. He cleared his throat and took a few steps toward the house.

"Can I interest you in coffee?" Marc held the back door open.

"That would be nice." Bria ran her hands through Brownie's fur. "I see the hot spots have healed. But you guys haven't been brushing him, have you?" Bria's disappointed tone pinched Marc's conscience.

"Miss Bria," Tyler's lower lip pushed forward into a pout, "Brownie cries so hard when we brush him."

"What kind of brush are you using?" Bria bent close to Brownie, finger-combing his back.

"Bring all of them." Marc called to Tyler's retreating form. "We have four. Brownie cries no matter which one we use."

Tyler gave the brushes to Bria. She chose a flat, oval brush with a rubber-gripped handle. Bria brushed the dog with expert strokes. "This is the best one. Brush him every day, then he won't need to be shaved down. His coat is beautiful." She pulled the brush through his fur. "Notice how he wants to pull away? It's because of the tangles." Bria rubbed his head, then gently brush Brownie's ears. "Even if you brush one part of him each day by the end of the week, his whole body will have been brushed at least once. After a while, he'll become accustomed to being brushed all over." She pulled a treat from her pocket. Brownie sat at attention, focusing on the treat. "Be a good boy." She slipped it into her back pocket and brushed Brownie. He stilled, transfixed on her pocket. She handed him the treat.

"Now, you try."

Marc stared at the brush. "Okay, but he hates me."

She handed Marc two treats. He fed one to Brownie, then placed the other on the counter nearby. Brownie stared at the counter. Marc brushed. Again, Bria's touch shot warmth up his arm as she corrected his method.

"Let me try." Tyler's request ended Marc's turn and put a safe distance between him and Bria. He handed his second treat to Brownie. As Tyler took his turn, Bria guided his hand. "Don't use treats as a constant reward," she said. "Insist he wait until you've brushed him thoroughly. Did you notice I gave him a treat during training while other times lots of affection? Affection has fewer calories and helps bond you all together in a way a treat will never do."

The coffee pot gurgled the end of the percolating cycle. Marc stood from his squat position near Brownie and gathered three mugs.

"How do you take your coffee?"

"With lots of milk."

"So do I," said Tyler as he climbed up on a stool.

"You're a little young for coffee." Bria looked between the two.

"Grammie gives him milk-coffee—a bit of coffee in a cup of warm milk. She served me the same thing as a child. So, I couldn't say no."

"My brother loved that when he was small. I never developed a taste for coffee until I was an adult." Bria sipped her brew.

Relief filled Marc knowing she didn't think he was a terrible father because he let Tyler drink milk-coffee.

"I need to go." Bria set the half-finished coffee in the sink. "Got a big schedule at work tomorrow. I'll see you next week."

Tyler spun on the stool and reached up from his perch for a hug. "See you Tuesday."

She hugged him tight. "Don't forget to work with Brownie every day."

"And play outside with him," Tyler added as he jumped off the stool to stand by Bria.

The smile she gave Tyler made a chink in the armor around Marc's heart regarding his objection to her tattoos and added another check mark on the pro side of his maybe dating her list. Bria gathered her phone and keys.

"I can walk you home." Marc hoped his voice sounded matter of fact.

"No worries, it's only a few blocks. Thanks for the offer." She waved at Tyler and headed out the door. Marc stepped onto the front porch as she proceeded down the sidewalk. He didn't move until she turned up her own driveway. *I'm only making sure she gets home safe.* Admitting he enjoyed her company was more honest. Was he willing to risk his heart—and Tyler's—on a stranger?

5

"Daddy, I need to see Miss Bria." Tyler opened Marc's office door. Marc focused on the computer screen. His son knew the rules. The door clicked closed and a long series of knocks followed. "Daddy, I need to talk to you. It's important."

"Come in." Marc turned his chair around and spread his arms, leaning forward for a hug.

Tyler stood in the doorway. "Please, come and see."

Marc followed him, disappointed at not receiving Tyler's hug. The website update his client wanted wasn't going well. They'd sent back the three designs he'd configured for them. *If they knew what they wanted, I'd be finished by now.* Grammie had volunteered to keep Tyler entertained while he finished his design. He hated giving up his Tyler time for clients, but he needed to earn a living.

His son's small hand clasped his as he pulled Marc toward the kitchen. "Grammie bought me clay." He pointed to the table. "I made Brownie."

A plump dog-shape made of green clay with a red head and tail stood lop-sided on the table.

"Nice job, Scooter."

Tyler beamed under the praise. "Can I give it to Miss Bria?"

"It needs to dry, honey." Grammie used a wet cloth to wipe the bits of clay from the table. "Maybe in a few days."

Marc gave her a smile and added, "How about we take it to her after school on Friday?"

"But...." Tyler's lower lip quivered.

"Young man, stop that this instant." Grammie waited until he looked at her. "Do you want the clay to fall apart before you can give it to her?"

"No." Tyler glanced at his creation, then back to Grammie.

"Clay needs time to dry. Grab the box." Grammie showed him the directions and they read them together. Marc appreciated his grandmother's teaching moments. She'd done the same for him when he'd struggled with reading when he was a child. Grammie and Granddad had filled the gap his parents' deaths had left. Now she was helping Tyler.

She pointed at the words. "What does it say?"

"Help me, Grammie."

"Allow," she began.

"One day ..." He looked at her.

"...before painting." Grammie finished.

Tyler smiled. "Can we paint it brown?"

"Of course. Add another day for the paint to dry. What day would that be?"

"Friday." Tyler smiled and watched Grammie place his creation on a shelf near some pig figurines. "Daddy, can we take it to Miss Bria on Friday?"

"You bet. We can go right after school." Marc ruffled his son's hair. "But if you don't get all your homework finished by Friday, we can't go."

"I'll do it now." Tyler raced to his backpack and brought his phonics practice cards to Marc. "Will you help me?"

He wanted to say, "I'm busy," but repeating his past failures would only hurt them both. Time away from his project would give him a fresh perspective. The two sat at the table and reviewed sounds, while Brownie snuggled at their feet. Tyler read books to him and together they played a math game. By the time they finished, Grammie served dinner. Some of the accumulated guilt from the past melted away with these precious times with Tyler.

LATER, Marc added his amen to Tyler's as he tucked the covers around his son. "What was your favorite part of today?"

Tyler's forehead creased, as it always did when he was considering his answer. Grammie had started this tradition long ago. Marc realized his grandmother had used it to set his mind on pleasant thoughts before bedtime.

"Doing homework with you, Daddy." Tyler reached up and Marc leaned in for the hug his son offered. "I don't want to do schoolwork when I'm not at school. You make it so fun. Can you help me instead of Grammie?" Tyler giggled and added, "She's okay, but you're more funnier."

"Sure." Marc got an extra hug. He pulled his son's arms off his neck and tucked them under the covers. "There may be days I can't, though."

"'Cause of deadlines?" Tyler scowled and signaled for Brownie, who rested his head on the edge of the bed. He stroked the dog.

"Smart boy." Marc chucked him gently under the chin. The smell of bubble gum shampoo still lingered from his morning shower. Once Tyler made eye contact, Marc said, "But I promise to not make it too often." He kissed Tyler's forehead.

"Okay." Tyler smiled and kissed his cheek.

Marc started to rise, but Brownie placed his head in Marc's lap. He patted the dog, who then gave him permission to leave by moving aside. Seems the dog needed a good night pat. He shook his head and headed for the door.

"Night, son."

"Night." Tyler turned on his side and Brownie jumped onto the bed to join him. The boy draped his arm around the mutt. Marc switched off the light, and headed back to his office. Helping with homework had been fun for him too, and seeing his son growing as a normal boy brought him hope. Could this one small sacrifice of his time aid Tyler in becoming a boy full of confidence and trust? Marc raked his mussed hair and prayed for Tyler's future and his current project.

Bria swept away dog hair from around her table as Aaron's baritone voice joined the overhead music. Bursting into song seemed to be her brother's go-to for stress-relief. Bria laughed when Aaron began dancing to "Uptown Funk" on the radio. He danced across the floor toward her with his last client, Bruno, a Saint Bernard. Aaron used a quick slide step as he held the dog's collar and escorted him to a crate.

"Come on, Bruno, keep up." Aaron tugged on the reluctant dog's leash as he stood stoic near the crates.

"Here we go." Bria grabbed a treat and got Bruno's attention long enough to get him in the crate. The dog huffed and plopped down on the floor. Aaron nodded, then he let loose with a series of steps. He wiggled his eyebrows at her.

"Let me show you how it's done." She giggled and caught the rhythm of the music, matching some dance moves she'd learned from video shots and high school musical chorus lines.

They'd done lots of impromptu dancing as kids. Joining him broke up the day and reminded her why she partnered with her crazy brother. She followed his lead as he improvised moves. Jazz hands didn't quite fit the tempo, but neither of them cared. When the music ended, they joined hands and bowed.

Applause filled the room. Marc and Tyler stood near the door. Bria blushed, and Aaron laughed.

"And now for my encore, I'm bathing Hamilton, the Great Dane who's afraid of water." Aaron headed to the bathing room.

"Miss Bria, you are a good dancer." Tyler's sweet smile erased her embarrassment.

"What do you have there?" Bria focused on the box as a change of subject from her silly dance moves.

"A surprise for you." He handed her the box.

She placed it on the reception counter and opened the flaps. "Oh, Tyler." She pulled out the painted creation. "Is this Brownie?"

"You guessed it." Tyler hugged her. "It's not the right color of brown."

"I love it." She smiled and placed it on Aaron's trophy shelf as whines echoed from the bathing room.

Marc shook his head. "Poor Hamilton."

Bria waved her hand. "He'll be fine. But poor Aaron, he'll have to change clothes. Our tub barely holds the dog. Horse would be a better description. Hamilton is on record as one of the largest of his breed." Bria prattled on about Great Danes, as the nervousness overtook her.

"Can I see Hamilton?" Tyler asked. "I've never seen a Great Dane."

"Miss Bria's busy." Marc came up behind his son and placed his hands on his shoulders. "And we don't want to interrupt Mr. Aaron."

Tyler flashed adorable, sad puppy-eyes at his father. Marc sighed and grinned at Bria. She tried not to melt into a puddle.

"Hamilton loves people." Bria stepped to the back-room door. "Mr. Aaron, Tyler would like to meet Hamilton."

"Give me ten minutes to dry... ahhh...stop shaking, dude." Aaron's chuckle carried to the front office. "Once he's dried, I'll let you introduce him."

"I've got chocolate chip cookies in the break room. Would you guys like some?"

"Yes, please." Tyler clapped his hands together.

Bria looked to Marc. "I should have asked you first. Would it be alright?

"Sure." Marc helped Tyler remove his backpack.

"Is he allergic to nuts?"

"No. Just no control with sweets." He turned to Tyler and held up a finger. "Only one."

"Daddy, can't I have two, please?" Tyler's cute plea met a shake of Marc's head and a look Bria had seen on her own father's face. It broached no argument. Tyler sighed and said no more.

Bria brought Tyler one cookie on a birthday-party paper plate.

"Whose birthday is it?" Tyler asked before taking a big bite.

"No one's. When the party store went out of business, we bought tons of paper plates."

"I actually designed their new online-store website." Marc took a purple princess napkin from Bria and wiped Tyler's face. "The owner sold more supplies online than in his storefront."

"Lots of stores are going online." Aaron led Hamilton out. "But you can't order a groomed dog online."

"Wow!" Tyler stared at the giant dog from behind Marc. The dog towered over Tyler.

Aaron handed the leash to Bria. "I'll be right back to do his nails."

Bria petted Hamilton, and he leaned into the attention. His head rested on her shoulder. "See, Tyler, he's just a big baby."

Tyler approached, the top of his head barely reaching the black dog's shoulders. "What do I do?"

"Hold out your hand."

Bria held the leash taunt, so Hamilton knew to be still. Tyler reached up. Hamilton sniffed his hand. "Nice dog."

Bria slackened the leash. Hamilton bent down and licked Tyler's face.

"Eww!" Tyler marched in place with his hands out. Slobber dripped on the floor. Marc grabbed a towel and wiped his son's face. Tyler calmed when the last remnant of the dog's lick was removed, his eyes a mixture of fear and curiosity.

Hamilton nuzzled Marc's hand. He petted the massive head that rested near his elbow. "See, he's not scary." The tremor in his voice didn't convince Bria.

Tyler grinned.

Hamilton lowered his head, and the boy scratched the monster between the eyes. The dog nestled closer, and Tyler stroked his head, patted his back, and then gave Hamilton a hug. "As long as you don't lick me, we can be friends."

"You can train a dog not to lick your face." Aaron entered the room wearing a smock with the Chicago Bears logo on it. "Bria can teach you."

"Brownie only licks my face a little." Tyler patted the Great Dane again, then took Marc's hand. "I like Brownie's kisses."

Marc squeezed Tyler's hand and looked toward Bria. "Brownie isn't much of a licker, but can you show us how to stop him from coiling himself around our legs?"

"Really, he does that?" Aaron squirted hand sanitizer into his palms and placed the bottle back on the counter. "My guess is he was raised with cats."

Bria added, "A firm 'no' should do the trick." She enjoyed their company but didn't want to waste time training Brownie to stop behaviors they could work on themselves. "An authoritative 'no' solves most behavior issues."

Aaron nodded. "If you pet him when he shows affection in other ways, he'll stop wrapping himself around your legs." He nudged Bria with his elbow. "Sis, this is my last dog, and your schedule is empty. I'll close up."

"I can help." Bria knew he had ulterior motives. "It's my day to close."

"I've dumped my turn on you a few times." He winked. "Take the rest of the day off." Before she could object further, he'd taken Hamilton back to the grooming area.

"Want to come to Mouse Maze with us?" Tyler gave his father another puppy face. "Can she come with us?"

"If Miss Bria wants to eat greasy pizza and watch you play arcade games, then she's welcome to join us." He imitated his son's pleading eyes.

Bria laughed. Time with Marc, with Tyler along, seemed a safe next step. "I haven't been to the Mouse Maze since they called it Pirate's Cove."

"That's right. I forgot." Marc shook his head. "Wow! That takes me back. My grandparents took all their grandchildren twice a year. It was our Christmas and birthday presents all rolled into two fun days."

"How many cousins do you have?" Bria removed her smock and used hand sanitizer. She pulled a brush from her purse and ran it through her hair, using the mirrored wall behind the shelves to check it.

In the mirror's reflection, she saw Marc look at the ceiling, appearing to count. "Twenty."

She spun around. "Twenty?"

"My grandparents had six children." Marc gazed at her while she finished brushing her hair.

For a moment, she lost her train of thought. "Dad has no siblings and my mother's sister and her husband live in Italy. I have two cousins I rarely see."

"I got five cousins my age." Tyler added. "I see them at church every Sunday.

"How fun." Bria grabbed her purse.

Marc continued. "We're a big family. I have two uncles who are twelve and fifteen years older than me who married around the same time I did. When I married my senior year of college, they were closer to forty." Marc opened the door for Bria and took Tyler's hand.

A lump formed in Bria's throat at the prospect of spending time with a guy who might be looking for a new life partner.

He pulled the key fob from his pocket and unlocked the doors. Marc opened her door and then secured a protesting Tyler in his car seat.

"Daddy, Jonas has a booster seat. Why do I gotta use a baby chair?"

"Jonas is taller than you. When you've grown big enough, you can use a booster chair." Marc's gentle tone impressed Bria.

"Can we measure me when we get home?"

"Sure." Marc's voice faded as he closed the door and moved around to the driver's seat. Marc handed a bag back to Tyler and turned on a kiddie tunes CD. Bria had no experience with single dads. Were they all this attentive to their children? It appeared she was in the presence of one of the devoted ones.

What happened to his marriage? Why hasn't Tyler mentioned his mom? Is she still in their lives?

Where did that come from? Why did she care? Was she ready to put herself out there like Aaron suggested? If this evening fizzled, Aaron was to blame.

6

"No." Tyler whined from his chair along the wall at Mouse Maze.

Marc had corralled his son long enough to tie his shoes before heading home.

"We can come back another time." Marc's ears rang from the noise level.

"I don't want to go." Tyler grumbled as they headed to the car. Bria held Tyler's hand while Marc grabbed the bag of junk his son had accumulated playing arcade games.

"I want ice cream." Tyler pulled away from Bria and crossed his arms. "Grammie always takes me for ice cream. I want ice cream." He stretched the words out and stomped his foot.

"Tyler Jonathan Graham, there will be no ice cream. Get in the car." Marc clicked the key fob to unlock the SUV. Tyler stamped to the car door.

Marc glanced over to see Bria's reaction. Her expression remained neutral as she took the bag from Marc, and he fastened his son into his car seat.

"He gets cranky when he's tired." Marc apologized as he closed the back door.

"What kid doesn't?"

Marc closed her door and moved around to the driver's side.

"You handled it well," she said.

"Thanks. That means a lot." He pulled out of the parking lot. "It's easy for me to give in. The therapist and my grandmother remind me to give him boundaries."

"My parents were big on rules. I wished I'd have appreciated them when I was growing up." Bria pushed a loose hair behind her ear. "I'm going to just ask. Where's Tyler's mom?"

"She passed away." He kept his voice just above a whisper so Tyler wouldn't hear. Talking about his mom when he was in one of his moods only made things worse.

"I'm sorry. I just assumed."

"Most people assume I'm divorced." Marc glanced in the rearview mirror. Tyler's head rolled to the side as his eyes closed.

He glanced her way before looking back at the road. "Tell me, how did you get into dog-grooming?" He didn't want to ruin an enjoyable time by dredging up Janet.

"Aaron offered me a chance to rebuild my life when I bailed on modeling."

"You were a model?"

Bria grew quiet. "I was offered a modeling contract fresh out of high school. The biggest mistake of my life."

"How so?

Her shoulders sagged and she crossed fer arms over her chest.

"Let's just say between the paparazzi, the modeling agency, and my manager, my life was not my own. Working with my brother is much more fulfilling and fun."

"Yeah, impromptu dance numbers are definitely more fun."

Bria's musical giggle reminded him of the time as a kid he'd filled one of Grammie's crystal goblets with water and ran his finger over the lip. Her tinkling sound made him laugh along with her. Tyler mumbled from the backseat, then grew quiet.

"Aaron is a character and an awesome caring brother." Bria lowered her voice. "How about you? What did you do in your other life before you moved in with your grandmother?"

"I worked for Hartwell & Sons, the biggest advertising company in Chicago. After my wife died, I sold all I had to pay hospital bills." He skipped the part about legal fees and court judgments from the family of the teen she'd killed. "Great company, lousy insurance, so I had no choice. I started my web design and marketing company and moved to Sugar Hill. I much prefer working with small businesses than corporate America."

"I read an article in *Fortune* about Hartwell. He's... what... only twenty-five? How old is his son?"

"Let's see... maybe two now?" Marc glanced at her. "I left because I didn't want Tyler to have a father so busy chasing success, he couldn't make time for his son. Family has become the most important thing to me now." The darkness and passing streetlights shadowed her face, making her hard to read.

Bria turned to the window. "You passed my shop."

"Sorry. I forgot you left your car there. Hey, would you mind if I take Tyler home? Then I'll walk you home and take you to work in the morning."

There was a long silence before she answered. "I can walk myself home." Shadows masked Bria's expression. "I'll need you to pick me up no later than nine thirty."

Marc nodded and did a happy dance in his mind.

They pulled into the driveway, and Bria carried Tyler's things into the house. "See you tomorrow." Marc called over his shoulder as he carried Tyler to bed. She waved, flashing what seemed a guarded smile, and closed the front door behind herself.

Marc wished she'd let him walk her home. After laying his son on his bed, he removed the boy's shoes, then pulled the covers up. Waking him to change into pajamas and brush his teeth was a prelude to hours of cranky wakefulness. Tyler always woke up happy when his rest was undisturbed. Brownie curled up next to Tyler. Marc rubbed between the dog's ears, then turned on the nightlight and left the room.

He brushed his teeth and crawled into bed. Clicking on the TV remote, he found the last quarter of a hockey game. He didn't follow the game. Instead, he relived the evening.

Bria had three kinds of laughs, the crystal tinkle, a light-hearted laugh, and a loud snort when something was outrageously funny. Tyler brought out the snorts. Bria hung on his every word, and her laughter brought out the best in Tyler. He'd been well-behaved until he got tired.

She'd not judged Tyler for his fussiness. Janet always made these activities about her. She'd buy Tyler things he didn't need and feed him junk food until he threw up, then scold him for vomiting.

Bria encouraged him to eat slower. She engaged Tyler in conversation and took his hand so that he walked rather than ran to the next game. His son's eyes sparkled most of the evening.

Tomorrow morning, he hoped to find out more about Bria. Maybe he'd

Google her. Or maybe not. For now, he'd wait. Best to let her tell him what she wanted him to know. He wouldn't want her to Google the car accident until he was ready to tell her. If she found out before he explained, it might be the end of their budding relationship.

BRIA'S PHONE rang the moment she opened her door. "Hey, what's up?"

"How was your date?" Aaron's nosiness had no limit. Bria glanced at the clock as it chimed ten.

"Tyler and I had a great time."

"Hey, isn't the guy's name Marc? Oh—ha ha."

The sound of water running left dead space for a moment.

"What are you doing?" Bria pushed the door closed.

"Cleaning my Iguana's tank." Aaron's voice sounded further away. He'd put her on speaker phone.

"You couldn't have waited to call me in the morning?"

"Nah, I'd rather get the scoop right away. How was your date?"

"It wasn't a date. We focused on Tyler the whole time." Bria propped her phone under her chin as she fastened the three locks on her front door. She'd added two more after buying the house. She was still having horrid nightmares, and the additional locks helped her sleep. "He's a great kid, and Marc is a great dad. The noise in that place gave me a raging headache, and I walked home from their house because Tyler fell asleep in the car. And Marc forgot I'd left my car at the shop."

"Need a ride to work?"

"No. You've got the early appointments. Besides, Marc offered to take me."

"Score." Aaron snickered.

"You're worse than Chloe." Bria placed her purse in the closet.

"That's only because she didn't know about your date." A brushing noise drowned out the next sentence.

"Stop scrubbing, it echoes through the phone." Bria flicked on the overhead light. "Our sister doesn't know about my non-date?"

"That's what I said. Unlike Chloe and the rest of the female population, I don't live vicariously through your love life."

"I don't have a love life." *Not yet anyway.* "Thanks for keeping your thoughts to yourself." Bria kicked off her shoes near the door. "Hey, if you don't live vicariously, then why did you call?"

"Because I can." He chuckled again. "And checking to see he wasn't a jerk."

"Everything was fine, overprotective brother-of-mine." Bria yawned. "I'm headed to bed now. See ya, love ya." She disconnected before her brother could say more and placed her cell on the charger. Aaron had great radar regarding the men his sisters dated. He'd disliked Mitchell instantly. At first, she marked it off as big-brother paranoia. But he'd had no such reservations about Marc...

Maybe Marc deserved a chance. Maybe she did too.

7

The Java Hut Coffee Shop overflowed with people on their way to work. Marc stood behind a well-dressed businessman engrossed in texting.

"Can we move it along?" The obnoxious man cast a glare at the young woman ordering at the counter, then popped the phone in his pants pocket and crossed his arms. "Courtney, seriously, just place your order."

She flipped her long blond hair away from her face and turned, matching his glare. "I'm ordering for my boss." She placed one hand on her hip and the other touched her cheek. "Oh, that's your boss too." The clerk passed her a cardboard holder with four cups. She flipped her hair again, and gave the guy a saucy smile with sway of her hips. "See you later."

The man mumbled something unrepeatable and stepped up to the counter.

Marc didn't miss the nine-to-five hustle or the office drama. He'd come to the coffee shop hoping a change of venue would stimulate creativity. The Vibe website wasn't coming along. These clients had turned out to be more clueless than the last. He'd had to dig deep and learn all he could about the company's products to give their website a facelift with interesting content. If the "aha moment" didn't come soon on their end, he'd might have to persuade them to settle for one of the ideas he'd already offered them.

The line moved ahead and grew behind. *Man, my timing is so bad.* He readjusted his laptop bag.

"Hey, bro."

Marc turned toward the voice. Aaron Willis stood in line behind him with his muscular arms crossed over a pink sleeveless t-shirt. His tats contrasted with the poodle under a dryer emblazoned on the shirt.

"That's a great color on you." Marc smirked.

Aaron laughed and offered a firm handshake. "Bria ordered these tees. I ripped off the sleeves to make 'em more manly." He wiggled his eyebrows at Marc.

"Your guns make it work." Marc pointed at Aaron's bulging biceps.

"True." He laughed. "It's a chick magnet at the gym." Aaron looked up at the menu board as they neared the counter. "Can we share a table?"

"Sure." Marc hoped he wasn't staying long. He'd come to work. But hanging with Aaron might prove interesting.

"Do you work here a lot?" Aaron pointed at the laptop case.

"This is my first time. I have an office at home. But today my brain is four-wheeling back trails rather than staying on the road to the deadline."

Marc reached the counter and placed an order for a blond roast coffee and grabbed a chocolate muffin. Aaron ordered two medium nitro cold brews with a yogurt parfait and a blueberry muffin. They found a table in the back corner.

"That's a huge muffin." Aaron said.

"I've cut way back on sweets with Tyler, but a guy's gotta have his chocolate fix." Marc took a bite.

"And you tease me about my pink shirt." He grinned as he sipped his brew. "Isn't a chocolate addiction a girl thing?" Aaron took the lid off the yogurt. "I eat the yogurt between sips because this nitro cold brew bothers my stomach."

"Why two then?"

"Nitro doesn't come in large." Aaron yawned. "And I just left a youth group lock-in at church." He ate half his muffin in a single bite.

"You're brave, working with teens. Not my thing. And chaperoning a group overnight. No way. A feisty five-year-old is enough of a challenge."

"That's why I ordered this super-charged drink. Only three hours of sleep and I've got a full Saturday grooming schedule." Aaron finished the muffin, took a gulp of coffee, then picked up his spoon again. "What is it you do?"

"I create websites and ad campaigns for companies."

Watching Aaron eat reminded him of the time Brownie snatched a cupcake that fell on the floor. The treat was gone in seconds. Marc sipped his coffee lest he mention the observation. "Working from home gives me time with Tyler. My former job was a sixty-hour a week gig."

"Doesn't work for a single dad." Aaron took the lid off his cup and added two packets of sugar. He stirred it before meeting Marc's eyes. "I wanted to ask you something."

"Okay." Marc tried to read the strange expression on his face.

Aaron looked around like a spy about to deliver a secret message. "I'm just going to say it." He took another sip of coffee. "What are your intentions toward my sister?"

Marc tried to keep his response light. "Do I look like a guy with evil intentions?"

Aaron squinted. "I don't know you well enough to make that call." He shifted in his chair, and his elbow grazed the arm of a passer-by. The girl frowned at him. "Sorry." He looked back at Marc.

"Hey, you've got no worries." Marc didn't want this big dude on his bad side.

"I hope not." Aaron leaned forward.

"Ask my grandmother. She'll vouch for my character." Marc felt like a kid being interrogated by the principal.

Aaron grinned. "Hey, who'd argue with Mrs. Carter?" They laughed, clearing the tension away. "You'll find me very protective when it comes to my sisters. Bria may appear all-together, but she's frail. Her ex chewed her up and spit her out. After three years, the old Bria is back. Since she gave up modeling, I've never seen her date or even talk about a guy."

"We aren't dating." Marc maintained eye-contact. Was he ready to date Bria or anyone? Did he want to open his broken heart when it was finally healed? And what about.... "Let me ask you something." Marc sipped his coffee while he searched for the right words. If Aaron could be so blunt then he's just say it. "Is Bria a party girl?"

"What?" Aaron's laugh boomed. "Are you on crack? In the three years she's been home, the only partying she's done is coming out to the farm for family barbeques."

"My late wife was a party girl. When I met her, she had one tattoo, and by the time she died she had twenty. I know tats are no big deal, but Janet was obsessed with them." He didn't mention her obsession with the tattoo artist. Marc cleared his throat. "We married on a whim, and that's how she treated our marriage. Janet had a drinking problem, and well...."

Aaron clapped a hand over Marc's forearm. "I get it. But Bria's tats are symbolic." Aaron pulled his T- sleeve to the side and pointed to a purple orchid tattoo on his shoulder. "Bria and my baby sister Chloe both have this tat. It's in memory of our sister Brittany. Orchids were her favorite. She died her senior year in high school. Cancer. It was tough on the family, but it crushed Bria. They were identical twins." Aaron cleared the huskiness from his throat.

"Then why the bird on her arm?" Marc's doubts were fleeting, but he had to know.

"Ask her yourself." Aaron stacked his empty cups together and laid them on his tray with his other trash. "She'll be happy to tell you. Don't let past mistakes keep you two from getting together." He grinned at Marc. "You have my permission. You'd be good for her. You and Tyler."

Aaron headed toward the garbage bin near the exit. He deposited the trash and left. *Whose past was he referring too? Bria's or mine?*

Marc opened his laptop as the morning rush subsided and quiet replaced the din of voices. The awkwardness of Aaron giving him permission to date his sister still hung over him. It was so weird. In high school he'd dated one of the Horton girls and her father had sat on the porch cleaning his gun when he arrived for the date. Meghan said her dad cleaned it on all the girl's first dates because he loved to scare them into behaving. He'd hate to get on Aaron's bad side. "Father, don't let me mess this up if it's something You have for me." He opened his Bible app and spent a few minutes reading Psalms one. "Trust in the Lord with all your heart...."

Yep, Lord, trust is a hard thing for me. He closed his laptop and headed to the car. Apparently, working on the website was not the reason he needed to be at the coffee shop. Maybe he should test the waters soon. Grammie would be thrilled to babysit if he asked Bria on a date. How would he keep Tyler from coming along? He was already enamored with her. First, he needed to ask her out, then he'd deal with his son.

～

MARC WAVED Bria to his table. He'd arrived early, too nervous to wait at home any longer. He'd set their coffee date until after Tyler was in bed. Grammie insisted coffee was always a safe, get-better-acquainted date.

Bria's multicolored, pastel skirt swayed as she approached, and her lavender top clung in all the right places. Her dark brown hair fell in waves around her shoulders. She pushed a strand out of her eyes, revealing a feathered earring, and the movement caused her charm bracelet to tinkle. Her welcoming smile melted some of Marc's nervousness.

A fruity scent greeted him as Bria slid into the chair. "Sorry I'm late."

"You're right on time. Tyler was so exhausted from chasing Brownie around the yard he fell right to sleep. Thanks for joining me so late."

"I was off today." She reached for a menu. "Whenever we have a super light day, one of us can stay home. It was my turn."

Bria pursed her lips as she skimmed the dessert menu. "So many choices."

"I looked at the menu while I waited for you. I'm having a brownie turtle sundae."

Bria looked over the menu at him. "Your favorite?"

"It's chocolate. And it's outstanding." Marc returned her smile. He wiped his sweaty palms on his jeans. "How was work?" Marc's neck warmed. "Sorry... you said you're off today."

The server approached and took their orders.

"Let me start over." Marc cleared his throat. "Thank you for coming."

Bria shifted in her chair and crossed her long legs. Marc noticed the three-inch heels on her sandals, then moved his eyes back to her gorgeous face. She shook her head and pushed the hair away from her face again. "This is the get-to-know-each-other, not-a-date-date." Bria leaned her left elbow on the table, placed her hand under her chin, and winked at him. The tips of his ears warmed. Great, he even reacted like a high school sophomore. That was the last time he'd nearly blushed in the presence of a girl.

"It's less awkward with a label on it." Marc shook his head. "I like that about you."

"Labeling?" Bria unwrapped her silverware from its napkin.

"No, your frankness." Marc smiled and unwrapped his own silverware. "It's refreshing."

"I prefer honesty. So, I'll start by saying my brother made me come." Her giggle took the sting out of the remark. "I'm comfortable with you, so let's see how this coffee-dessert thing goes."

"First, I have a question that's been nettling me."

"You want to know about my phoenix."

"Phoenix?"

She flipped her left arm over to display a bird rising from the ashes. "Aaron said he explained Brittany's orchid."

These siblings are tight. The sadness in Bria's eyes made him wished he hadn't asked about the bird tattoo.

"Brittany and I were close." Bria fiddled with her paper napkin. "As identical twins, we could read each other's minds." She offered a weak smile. "She was smarter, classier, and more confident than me. A modeling agency wanted to sign her. Brittany thought it was a great way to earn college tuition." She lined the utensils atop her napkin. "Brittany had a couple of photo shoots and then she got cancer."

"I'm sorry." Marc offered.

She shrugged, her emerald eyes reflecting her loss.

"Our senior year of high school was the hardest. She was sick from chemo treatment and had to drop out of everything. If I wasn't at school, I was with Brittany. She seemed to recover and talked about getting back on the runway. Then something went wrong with her med cocktail, and Brittany's heart gave out. She passed away while the family was at my graduation." Bria took a deep breath. "Anyway, I got this crazy idea to fulfill Brittany's dream. I contacted her modeling agency, took their classes, and spent five years traveling the world as Brittany. My ex was my manager. I looked in the mirror one day and realized I hated the person I'd become."

Marc searched his mind for the right response, not wanting to sound cheesy. "It looks like you turned your life around." He squeezed her hand then removed it. *That sounded cliché.*

"This phoenix," she pointed to the bird, "covers the tattoo of my ex-boyfriend's name. It represents my new life rising from the ashes of my old life because Jesus redeemed me."

Shame covered his heart. This beautiful woman wasn't his ex-wife. "Janet's goal was to cover herself with tats." He took a bite of his dessert, it tasted like sand as he recalled his late wife. "She cheated on me with her tattoo artist."

The server brought their desserts. Marc blessed their food, then took a bite, waiting for Bria to respond to his confession. Berating him for being a woose, just like Janet. But Bria ate her berry pie à la mode without a word.

"My late wife preferred partying to marriage. Janet enjoyed her pregnancy and read child rearing books. That gave me hope she'd settle down. Then Tyler cried a lot, and Janet said, 'He's too needy.'" As soon as I came home from work, she went off with her friends. Every week she was either talking about getting a new tattoo or getting one."

"Not everyone with a tattoo is...."

"I know, there were people at work with sleeve tattoos. But my experience with her taught me otherwise. Janet drank heavily and stayed out late. When she left last year, she took Tyler. Her plan was to hit me up for a large alimony payment and child support."

"Surely not." Bria touched his hand as her eyes reflected sympathy.

"She also said Tyler was a mistake. A mistake I would pay for until he was eighteen." Marc's dessert had turned to mush. He stirred it. "She rode away intoxicated and took a curb too hard, and her life ended along with a teen driver. Tyler was in the backseat. I'm so thankful she secured him in his car seat... I'd have lost my mind without him."

They finished their desserts in silence. Marc focused on the soft background music playing in the restaurant. What possessed him to bare his heart like that. No one but Grammie knew the truth.

Bria broke the silence. "So, what's your favorite color? Mine's pink."

Marc studied her face for a moment. Her gentle smile chased the heaviness from his heart. "Orange."

"Orange?"

"Yeah, and navy blue. Go Chicago Bears."

Marc laughed at her groan. Light-hearted questions and cute stories from their childhood filled the rest of their evening. The server brought their check and cleared the table long before they were ready to go.

"Can you pay your check so I can go home?" the manager called from the cash register. Bria's blush matched Marc's own embarrassment. They walked to Bria's car and chatted for a while longer. When the restaurant manager locked up and left, Marc moved toward his car. "This was great."

"I have early appointments tomorrow. Want to go hiking Sunday afternoon?"

"Sure." He hadn't been since I was a Boy Scout. "I'll check to see if Grammie has any plans, then I'll confirm with you."

"Sounds good." She slid into her Prius, and he followed her home. He pulled in front of her house and waited for her to go in. She waved, and he drove up the street to his home. Grammie had left the porch light on, but the rest of the house was dark. He glanced at the dashboard clock. "Midnight!" Time stood still in Bria's presence. Marc was alert, his adrenaline spiked. He headed to his office. If he could distract his mind from the photographic review of every minute with Bria, he might get some sleep before Tyler woke up.

8

"**M**iss Bria! Miss Bria!" A loud knock on her front door accompanied the small voice. Bria opened the door to a tearful Tyler. "Brownie is gone."

"Did he dig a hole under the fence again?" Bria had hoped he'd be content in his yard by now.

"No, he ran away." Tyler hiccupped.

"Surely not." Bria held out her arms, and Tyler cuddled close. She kissed his hair and cooed to calm the river of tears. She carried him to the sofa. Holding the boy felt as natural as breathing. A sad pang beat inside. If not for the miscarriage.... She refused to think on the past.

"Where was Brownie when he ran away?"

"Julian's house."

"Who's Julian?"

"My friend from school. Grammie dropped me off there to play. He has a dog too."

"Does Julian have a fenced-in yard?"

"Yes. But the fence is shorter than ours because Julian has a chiwawee."

"A chihuahua," Bria corrected, handing over the box of tissues from the end table. He blew his nose and then snuggled close again. She pushed his bangs out of his eyes. "Tell me what happened." Bria looked at the wall clock and disengaged Tyler to send a quick text to Aaron.

"Julian always takes Pedro to the dog park. We took Brownie too. Dogs can run free there." Tyler lowered his head. "Julian and I were looking at a dead bird Pedro found. Brownie ran away then ." He sobbed again. Bria rubbed his back. As she comforted the child, it stirred the longing she'd buried. She lifted his chin to get eye contact.

"Then what happened?"

"We looked all over the park. Julian's mom and brother helped me look. Mrs. Martin called Grammie, and she picked me up. I ran here right away 'cause you know how to find him."

Bria sighed. Her late work start would be later still. "Where's your dad?"

"At home, I guess."

"Tyler, you can't just come here without telling your dad or Grammie."

"Grammie saw me leave." The boy's logic and serious expression forced her to stifle a laugh. She didn't want to encourage his rash behavior.

"Let's go talk to your dad." She took his hand.

"But he's not good at dog stuff like you are." Tyler's confidence touched her.

She opened the front door to find Marc standing there.

"Grammie said he ran this way." He squatted in front of his son. "You can't run off without telling anyone. I know you're upset, but you need to wait for me."

"I'm sorry. Miss Bria said that too. But we need to find Brownie quick. He might be hurt or starving."

"I doubt he's starving." Marc ruffled his hair. "We'll find him." He stood and smiled at her. "Well, great and mighty dog whisperer, what do we do?"

"Thanks for the flattery." Her pulse quickened with his smile. "You can make posters, and I'll put his information on the town Facebook page."

"There's a town Facebook page?"

She found Marc's confused expression endearing. "Really, you don't know that, being a web designer and all. You'd be amazed at how fast they assimilate information in these groups. The last time there was an in-store sale at Walmart, it got posted on the site. An hour later, the item was sold out." Bria tapped on her phone.

"We'll put it on the neighborhood page too." She showed him the link. "Send me a picture of Brownie to post. I gave them the shop phone number so that way no one will have your personal number. Put the shop address on the poster. If anyone finds him, the shop is a better option to return Brownie."

"If he's gotten into something, like greeting a skunk, you can bathe him." The tension left his face. "Thanks." He placed his hand on Tyler's shoulder. "Come on. Let's go make posters, then we'll put them everywhere." He turned back to her. "Great Saturday activity."

She nodded in sympathy.

~

"Daddy, this is really cool." Tyler stared at the lost dog poster. "A nice person will find Brownie and bring him to Miss Bria's shop. He'll be home soon."

"Absolutely." His words held more confidence than he felt. If Brownie wasn't found, he dreaded the drama that would follow. "Let me print off a bunch of copies, then we'll head out."

Tyler held the posters while Marc taped them to poles and store sign boards. By lunch, they'd covered several blocks. "Daddy, I'm hungry."

Marc scooped up Tyler and set him piggyback on his shoulders, then carried the bag of posters and supplies as they headed home. "Let's see what Grammie has for lunch."

"Daddy," Tyler patted Marc's head, missing his eye by inches. "Daddy, what if Brownie is so lost we never find him?"

What do I say, Father? He didn't want to give him false hope. "He's a smart dog, he'll find his way home. It just might take a while."

"He is smart. I'll pray God tells him how to find our house." Tyler straightened and pulled leaves off the trees near the sidewalk. A branch smacked Marc on the shoulder. "Sorry, Daddy." Marc moved Tyler to the sidewalk to avoid further head injury.

The mark on his face stung, it would probably swell. Just what he needed to make this day perfect.

~

The doorbell bonged. Bria finished taking a payment from a customer as the pungent smell of body odor filled the room. Brownie stood next to a man wearing a tattered camouflage jacket, faded jeans, and an Army Strong ball cap. His long graying hair and beard framed friendly eyes. He kneeled beside the dog and stroked his face, then rose and faced her.

"Ma'am, I'm returning Brownie." He signaled for the dog to go. Brownie stared at him. "Jack, sit." The dog complied with a tongue-drooping smile.

Bria watch the interaction as the man motioned for Brownie to heel. His chin quivered, but he remained in a parade-rest position.

"He was your dog?" Bria came around the counter.

"Yes Ma'am." He patted Brownie. "When I lost my home, he lived with me on the street. Winter will be here soon and shelters won't take dogs. I'd hoped he'd found a good home."

"Oh, he has." Bria extended her hand. "I'm Bria Willis. Tyler is anxious to get him back."

"Lloyd Harmon."

Aaron came out from the back room. "I see you found Brownie."

"Brownie used to belong to him." Bria related to the man's loss. When Clarence died, she'd been crushed. She couldn't imagine what it must be like to give your friend away.

"Except I called him Jack." Lloyd squatted and scratched Brownie's head, then Brownie rolled over for a belly rub. "I'm sorry for worrying the child. Jack found me, and...." He rose and adjusted his cap on his head. "I thought it was a sign. I'd been praying for God to open doors. He knew I was missing Jack. When he found me, I thought maybe...?" He cleared his throat and offered a half-smile. "The good Lord knows what's best for me and for Jack. A little visit was nice. Now it's time for him to get on home." He turned to leave. Compassion sprung an impulse into Bria's mind.

"Wait." Bria called. "Are you good with dogs?"

"You could say that. I was in the K-9 unit in the Army." Lloyd resumed a parade-rest stance.

"Would you like a job?" Aaron followed her lead. Hope filled the man's eyes, then faded.

Lloyd's head drooped. "I got to tell you I have PTSD. Most people assume I'm violent." He stroked Brownie again. "I grew up around dogs. My dad bred German Shepherds and trained them for the police. My PTSD makes me depressed, and sometimes I have panic attacks."

"I know PTSD is misunderstood." Bria's doctor had diagnosed her with a mild case of it from her own trauma.

"If you're not opposed to washing dogs, I'll take you on for a trial period." Aaron extended his hand.

Lloyd grinned and shook both their hands. "I'm obliged. Seems Jack coming to me was a sign after all. I washed my dad's dogs as a kid. Tell me how you want it done, and I'll do my best."

"You start Monday. I'll have a t-shirt for you."

Lloyd looked at himself. "I'll cleanup and be ready to work." Then he opened the door and turned. "Thanks."

Brownie started for the door, but Bria restrained him. She wrinkled her nose. "It's a bath for you." Brownie put his paw over his eyes.

Aaron laughed and clicked a lead to his collar. "I'll bathe him while you call Marc with the good news."

~

TYLER HUGGED Brownie as soon as Aaron brought him out of the back. "Don't never, ever scare me again."

Marc pulled his wallet from his pocket. Bria held up her hand. "Don't. Seeing Tyler's happy face is payment enough." Before he could protest, she inserted playfully, "This time."

"I wish we could meet the guy and thank him."

"You can. Lloyd is homeless, so we hired him as a bather. He starts Monday."

"No background checks?" Marc shook his head.

"He's a veteran and served with the K-9 unit." Aaron came to her defense.

"My brother has great instincts about people. Besides, this guy loved and trained Brownie, yet gave him back for Tyler's sake. A guy like that has redeeming qualities in my book."

"Okay...it's none of my business." Marc offered a weak smile.

"Lloyd deserves a fresh start." Bria knew how important those could be. "It's on a trial basis for now. The weekend crowd will be the real test." She pulled a neckerchief from a shelf and tied it around Tyler's neck to match Brownie's.

Marc tugged on the neckerchief. "Next time, don't let him off the leash in the dog park until you have taught him his boundaries."

"Like the fence?" Tyler took the leash from Marc.

"Exactly."

"I promise." Tyler took his dad's hand.

"I'll take them to the park a few times." Marc nodded in her direction. "Thanks again for the trouble you took. We still on for hiking tomorrow?" His face held hope. *As if he thought losing Brownie was a deal breaker.*

She gave him a reassuring smile. "Come by the house about eleven. I'll drive."

"It's a plan." He smiled and placed his hand in Tyler's.

The sweet picture of the twosome hand-in-hand with their fluffy mutt reminded her of a greeting card. *Father, are these two supposed to be a part of my life?* Her prayer was interrupted by a yowly basset hound. The senior dog had joint issues. "Mortie, how are you today?"

The dog's teenage owner matched his slow pace. "Mortie takes his time getting places but he's a happy dude."

"Sean, Aaron is finishing up a groom. Go ahead and take Mortie back to a crate."

"Okay. Hey, can I ask you something?" Sean lowered his voice. "Do you think he'll be okay if I get a puppy?"

"Change can be hard for an old dog. It may take time for Mortie to warm up to a puppy. But over time, they'll be best friends."

"I hope so. I can't imagine not having a dog around." Sean took Mortie to the back.

Change *was* hard. When her collie died, she couldn't bring herself to get another dog. When she missed him, she went to Bowwow Rescue and played frisbee with the dogs.

Was she ready to have another man in her life, one with a ready-made family? Or was she playing a little frisbee to take the loneliness away? Tyler had already wriggled his way into her heart. But Marc was an addition she wasn't sure about.

Tomorrow would be another chance to dip her toe in change.

9

"Take these." Grammie held out Marc's grandfather's hiking boots. She'd polished the worn boots until they shined.

"No way." Marc felt like a teen arguing with her over the clothing styles of the cool and not-so-cool. "I bought new tennis shoes. I'll be fine."

"You'll thank me later." Grammie shoved the boots toward him.

Marc finished tying his new shoes. The salesman had recommended hiking boots too.... "I'll be fine. These are good quality walking shoes."

"Stubborn as always." Grammie cradled the boots in her arms. "I'll buy Epsom salts and Tiger Balm for your muscle aches."

"Thanks." Marc kissed her cheek, and she hugged him. "Tyler, come here."

Tyler and Brownie ran into the room, wearing their matching, bone-patterned neckerchiefs. Tyler had worn it to church, much to Marc's frustration. He'd feared the other kids would ridicule his son. Instead, his friends thought it was cool. Tyler was much bolder than Marc had been as a child. More of free-spirit and less concerned about what others thought. Which was both a blessing and an aggravation.

"Hey, Daddy, leaving now?"

"Yep, be good for Grammie." Marc retied the neckerchief. "I promise to be home before bedtime."

"You'll be with Miss Bria, so it'll be okay." Tyler hugged him again. "She doesn't drink and drive fast."

A rock lodged in Marc's stomach knowing Janet's drinking composed Tyler's most vivid memory of his mother.

"I'm going to play with Brownie all day and keep a close eye on him."

"Sounds like a plan." Marc blinked away moisture. Brownie was the best thing for his son. The mutt had brought happiness and peace back into his life. The two devoted friends would have a great day together. The usual guilt at leaving his son was nearly non-existent as he headed out. "See you later."

Tyler waved to him from the door as Marc walked toward Bria's with his backpack.

BRIA HANDED Marc her heavy pink backpack. "Put the packs in the trunk."

He touched the royal blue frame of her Prius. "You're taking this classy car into the woods?"

"It'll be fine in the parking lot." She appraised his appearance as he shut the trunk. He wore long sleeves and jeans. "You don't own any hiking boots?"

He pulled a ball cap from his pocket and put it on. "I bought these walking shoes for today."

"Haven't had time to break them in, I see." The shiny white exterior contrasted to his well-worn jeans.

"I'll be fine. These are top of the line, and the sales associate made sure they were the right fit.

"If you say so." Typical man, think they know everything. Her jaw tightened. "I'm driving."

"Of course, it's your car." Marc reached for the passenger door latch.

"Wise man." She gave him a bright smile. This concession balanced the scale against his poor choice in shoes. "My brother insists on driving everywhere, even if it's my car." So had Mitchell.

"Hey, my grandmother taught me to respect women." They slid into the car. "And I'm the same way. No one else drives my car." He ran his hand over the leather interior. "If I had a sweet ride like this, I'd be extra protective."

"So why don't you have a sweet ride?" Bria glanced at him before focusing on the road ahead.

"I did, a Mustang convertible." Marc shared the details of his baby. His voice softened and he looked her way. "After my wife crashed her car, I sold the Mustang. Tyler is safer in the SUV."

"You're a great dad to put Tyler's safety first."

"Someday I'll buy another one. Probably when I retire."

"Isn't that what all old guys do?" Bria teased.

"My grandfather bought a 1963 silver Mustang when he retired."

"I'm seeing a theme here." Bria flashed a smile.

"I guess I love Mustangs because they remind me of him." Marc stared out the passenger window. "Are we there yet?" His tone was an imitation of Tyler.

They both laughed. Bria's nervousness melted with the easy chatter. Marc was transparent, easy to relax around. She pulled into a parking space and pressed the button to open the trunk before she got out. Hilly woods surrounded the gravel parking lot. Signs indicated trails and their difficulty. A mother and son walked past with fishing gear. Mosquitos buzzed by their faces.

"Did you bring bug spray?" Marc collected the backpacks.

"Here." Bria handed him a disk. "Hook that fan to your waistband. It's wonderful for keeping mosquitos away."

Marc smelled it and crinkled his nose. "Does it work?'

"Like a charm." Bria pushed a button, and a tiny fan whirred, releasing the bug spray. Marc did the same and fastened it on the waist of his jeans.

"I'll trust you on this."

"We'll start with an easy trail." Bria headed out and Marc kept pace at her side, sidestepping hanging tree boughs.

"Don't make it easy on my account." Marc took her hand. Warmth spread through her. "I can keep up."

His blond hair peeked out around his cap, making him look younger. He squeezed her hand.

She jerked away, her delicious response to his touch unnerving. "Let's step over here and stretch."

"Okay." Marc didn't respond to her sudden distance. Instead, he followed her lead. "You hike a lot?" Marc extended his arms to the side and stretched.

His snug shirt revealed his lack of bulging biceps. Comparing him to Aaron was so ridiculous. What was wrong with her? It was better than comparing him to Mitchell. Who took Pilates and spin classes. *Stop it!*

What was his question? Oh, yeah—hiking. Bria stretched her arm over her head.

"As often as I can." She headed out on the trail, pumping her arms and keeping her pace brisk to avoid opportunity for hand holding. "Usually, I come alone."

"Isn't that dangerous?" Marc rolled his shoulder.

"It could be. When I say alone, I mean I meet a group of fellow hikers and we all put in earphones."

"How weird.... Sorry, I mean, do you even know these people?" Marc's concerned expression changed to anxiety as he stumbled over a tree root. He steadied himself. His face red, whether from the sun, exertion, or embarrassment, she couldn't decide. A cardinal called from a tree branch.

"I know them as my hiking buddies. We don't hang out." Her shallow relationship with the group equaled no drama. "They're addicted to hiking and set a good pace. I like the challenge." She stopped, lowered her backpack, and took a swig from one of the water bottles. She intended the break for Marc's benefit. Normally, she would have walked another mile before pausing to drink. "My hiking buddies got into a political argument during the election, and we voted no talking on the trail unless it was about the terrain ahead."

Marc looked winded, taking deep breaths and wiped sweat from his forehead with his sleeve, but he didn't complain. "What do you listen to while you hike?" Marc pulled off his backpack.

"Marches or audio books." Sharing her love for hiking with Marc was fun. Bria sensed this time with him was a new step toward the normal Aaron claimed she needed. She glanced at the attractive man keeping pace with her. The exhilarating feeling as she walked with him had little to do with her hobby and more to do with the man.

The sun crested high in the sky when they reached the end of the trail. Sweat soaked Marc's shirt. Bria wore a wick shirt that absorbed her perspiration, making her more comfortable. "Let's stop for lunch and then we'll head back."

Marc limped toward a nearby picnic table. Bria pulled out the first aid kit. "Your shoes bothering you?"

"I'm fine, just tired and hungry." He gave a dismissive wave, then pulled food from his backpack. "Grammie wouldn't let me see what she packed."

"It was so nice of her to provide lunch." Bria grabbed a banana, peanut butter crackers, and a container of trail mix.

"I was hoping for two sandwiches." Marc searched deeper in the backpack.

"She's a wise woman and an experienced hiker. Before your grandfather died, he took her hiking all the time."

"Grammie tried to get my wife and I to go hiking when we visited, when Tyler was a baby. Janet laughed at the idea, and we caught a movie instead." Marc finished a second banana.

"Maybe you can get Delores to start hiking again. It's an easy way to stay in shape and catch up on reading at the same time."

Bria had asked her last summer, and the pain in Delores' eyes had kept her from asking again. *Her grandson might be harder to say no to.* "It would give your grandmother more people to love on."

"For sure. That woman hasn't met a stranger. She'd get your hiking buddies chatting." His laughter came from deep inside, inviting her to join in. Marc gathered the trash and threw it in a nearby refuse container. "I'm ready when you are."

"How are your feet?" Bria began packing her backpack.

"Rested and ready to go." Marc smiled as he shuffled toward her.

"Are you sure?" She held the first aid kit before him. One last chance not to be macho-man.

"Let's get to it." Marc shouldered his backpack, and Bria zipped the first aid kit inside hers.

He was lying. His new shoes would have worked lots of blisters on his feet by now. "Let's take trail number four back to the parking lot. It's a fun climb with a great view."

MARC'S FEET screamed for release from his sneakers. He tried not to limp as the shoes rubbed over the tender spots forming on his heels. His left big toe and the side of his right foot ached. The path narrowed as the incline upward forced him to crawl. Bria disappeared over the ledge. Panic overtook him as he crept toward the top. "Bria." He hated the fear in his voice. "Bria."

She peered over the edge twenty feet above. "You can do it, Marc, I believe in you." Her words of encouragement did nothing to still his racing heart. The hard rock outcropping scratched his palms and his jeans were now stained with dirt and grass from his attempt to get to the top. She threw a rope to him. "Hang on, the other end is tied to a tree." Marc took the lifeline and pulled himself forward, his pride crushed under the humiliation of needing her help. At the top, he couldn't look Bria in the eyes.

Marc sat on a stump, his hand pressed against his chest as he searched for air. "Can we go home now?" Bria gave him a water bottle, and he gulped. "I deserved this."

"What do you mean?" Bria sat on the ground beside him.

"My feet are killing me. I have blisters on my blisters." He untied his shoes and peeled off his socks. "I didn't want to disappoint you."

"Disappoint me?" Bria examined his feet. "Ew, these are ugly." She grabbed her first aid kit and applied ointment and bandages to the blisters. "If you would have walked this entire trail in blisters, that would have disappointed me. Manly pride doesn't impress me." She administered the last band-aid. "Do you have fresh socks?"

"I think Grammie packed a pair." Searching through his bag he found socks at the bottom. "Wisdom strong in that one is." Marc attempted a Yoda impression.

Bria laughed so hard she snorted, then covered her mouth. As he laughed with her, his humiliation was erased. She took the socks and gently pulled them over the bandages. "Trail four is for experts. It's partly my fault, I'm sorry."

"I get it. My sister would test a guy's mettle on the wooden roller coaster at Six Flags" Marc tied his shoes, then stood beside her. "All is forgiven."

Without forethought, he brushed her full lips with a feather-light kiss. She tasted like peanut butter.

"I'm glad you don't like macho because I'm not good at it." He kissed her again, lingering longer. She relaxed, returned his kiss, then jerked away and took a step back. His pulse pounded. Had he misread her? Bria looked away, her hand pressed to her lips.

"We should get going." She cleared her throat as she packed the rope and her first aid kit in her backpack. Bria pulled it over her shoulders and took a deep breath as she glanced at her surroundings.

"I'm not looking forward to falling down the trail." To ease his nervousness, Marc looked for a long stick to support himself but found none.

"There's a shortcut to the parking lot through there." She pointed at an obscure path. "Logan, my hiking buddy, found it a few years ago. We'll have to walk across the creek on man-made stepping stones."

Marc followed her on a one-man wide trail through tall prairie grass. He glanced at the path often to avoid tripping on the ruts.

"You all right back there?" Bria turned as she stepped over a hole in the path.

"No worries." He offered a weak smile. and kept pace with her despite the pain. "How far?"

"We're at the creek now."

They moved into a small clearing. The park rangers had spaced oil drums filled with concrete across the creek for steppingstones. A few dipped at an angle.

"This is the only way?" Marc's panic waited backstage as he stared at the creek. "I can't swim."

"If you fall off the stones, it's only waist-high."

"Are you sure?"

"Aaron thought he'd race across the creek. He slipped in and got drenched. The bottom is slimy and slick. I have a video of his hulky self stumbling to the other side. I threaten to post it on YouTube when he gets obnoxious."

Marc watched Bria step effortlessly across the stones. He followed much slower, gauging each concrete circle. On the third of the six, his foot slid. He squeaked and flayed his arms. Moving his foot to the left, he found drier concrete and a steady perch. He took the next two stones with his heart in his throat. On the last stone, his foot skidded to the edge. He righted himself, leaped to the other side of the creek, and landed on his backside.

Bria slid her phone into her pocket and applauded.

"You recorded that?" Marc cringed as he rose from the dirt.

"Absolutely. Aaron needs to see how a real man does things the safe way." Her compliment took away the sting of his awkwardness. She grabbed his hand and pulled him through a copse of trees. "Watch out for low-hanging branches." Bria maneuvered through the thick foliage, tugging him behind her.

Marc crouched more than he stood, afraid of whacking his head. The scratch he got during his walk with Tyler was still visible. In a few minutes they exited the woods on the other side of the parking lot. "Free at last."

Bria laughed, handing over another water bottle. He downed half, then took her hand as they walked to the car. "Glad you drove. My feet can't wait to escape captivity." He kicked off his shoes once in the passenger seat. "My toes thank you."

"Don't wear shoes the next few days. Be sure to soak in a hot bath. Stretch all the other parts of your body that will ache tomorrow." Bria leaned over and kissed his cheek. "Thanks for coming. I'm sorry about the blisters."

"But you're not," he teased.

"Maybe just a little." She pinched a tiny bit of space between her thumb and forefinger. There was something behind the sparkle in her eye that drew him. He leaned in and kissed her as if she'd not moved away from his first attempt. This time, she placed her arms around his neck and ran her fingers through his hair, returning his ardor. Deeping the kiss he bumped the stick shift, sending pain through his knee. "Oww."

"You all right?" Bria touched his leg, then burst out laughing. "Stay on that side of the car, Mr. Graham. I don't want to explain to the ER doctor how you got your injury.

"Kissing a beautiful woman." Marc leaned in again, but she shifted gears, causing his head to connect with the window. "Hey, unconscious isn't a good look." Marc rubbed his head.

"I am so sorry." She struggled to keep a straight face, but a giggle erupted from her lips.

They laughed and spent the rest of the trip home discussing silly stunts from their childhood. Before Marc was ready to end their date, they pulled into Grammie's driveway. He debated stealing another kiss when the auto-unlock button clicked on his door.

"I'll see you Tuesday night." She'd made the decision for him.

Bria stifled another laugh as Marc hobbled from the car, shoes in hand, and closed the door. This guy was so different from anyone she'd ever known. When he tapped on her window, she shrieked and then rolled it down. He leaned inside, his boyish grin sent a rush of warmth through her. Was he going to attempt another kiss? Did she want him to?

"I had a great time. Once my feet recover, we can try again."

"Sounds like a plan." Bria refrained from using the word, "date." She drove the few blocks to her home and noticed Marc waiting in his driveway, watching her. She waved, and he headed inside his house. His need to see that she got into the house safely was both sweet and unnerving.

Mitch had watched her too.

It seemed like Marc had different motives, so risking a relationship with him might not send her tumbling into a dark abyss.

10

B ria looked up from the computer as the doorbell tinkled. Delores Carter held the door for Tyler and Brownie. "Hello, Miss Bria. It's time for Brownie's haircut." It had been two weeks since the hike, and Marc had called or texted her every day since. Yesterday, he'd asked her out for dinner this coming Saturday and the thought made her heart skip a beat. How she wished Marc had come with them.

Tyler's eyes sparkled as he reached for her.

Bria pulled the boy close. Tyler squeezed hard before releasing her. "Brownie misses you. Can we have more lessons?"

"The boy is anxious to teach Brownie new tricks." Delores hugged Bria's shoulder, then held out a plastic bag. "Muffins."

"Thanks. Aaron and Lloyd will love these."

"Whose Lloyd?" Delores asked.

"Our new bather,"

"Brownie used to be his dog." Tyler's face fell with worry.

"Now, young man don't you worry." Delores hugged Tyler close. "Brownie is your dog now."

"Lloyd, come out here." Bria stood near the door to the bathing room. A clean-shaven version of the veteran greeted Brownie.

"How's my boy?" Lloyd scratched the dog's muzzle and in moments Brownie flopped on his back for a thorough belly rub. "That's my good boy."

"Lloyd, let me introduce Tyler's grandmother, Delores Carter."

Lloyd grinned up at her. "Nice to meet you, ma'am." He turned to Tyler. "I see you're taking good care of Jack."

"Yes, he's my best friend." Tyler chewed his lower lip as the two played.

"Lloyd, that dog hates baths. Is your strategy to fool him with belly rubs?" Bria laughed. "Are you sure he'll get in the tub now?"

"No problem, ma'am." Lloyd rose and signaled Brownie. The dog heeled near his old master. The man looked at Tyler. "Son, you got no worries about me taking your best friend."

Relief flooded Tyler's face.

"But I'd like for him to see my new place. Can you bring him by?"

"Sure." Tyler looked over at Grammie. "Can you take me there?"

Delores looked at Bria before answering. She nodded in approval. Bria had found Lloyd to be an excellent employee with a kind heart.

Delores smiled and asked, "Where do you live?"

"Upstairs. They've kindly let me stay in the one-bedroom apartment over the shop rent-free for renovating it."

"I'm embarrassed he lives in the middle of the construction mess." Bria appreciated the man's talents. When she'd purchased the building, Aaron's priority was the shop. He'd planned on renovating the apartment for himself, but life got too busy once Doggie Designer Duo opened.

"After living in a cardboard box, upstairs is a mansion." Lloyd patted Brownie's head.

"Cool!" Tyler said, then turned to Bria. "Can you teach me an extra special cool trick?"

"Ty has talked about nothing else since Marc signed the permission slip for the school talent show," Delores explained.

"If Brownie learns a special trick, we could win first place." Tyler scratched between Brownie's eyes.

"I got one." Lloyd smiled. "Jack...Brownie already knows it." He took off the dog's leash. "Fire, fire!" he yelled. Brownie woofed.

"Stop."

The dog crouched.

"Drop."

He laid flat.

"Roll."

He rolled over a few times.

"Evacuate!"

Brownie crawled to the door.

Tyler clapped. "Mr. Lloyd, that's so cool."

Tyler called Brownie and practiced the routine with him. The dog repeated each step. Tyler gave him a treat from the bowl on the counter. "Awesome."

Lloyd signaled to Brownie to heel. "Time for a bath." Brownie whimpered, but followed.

"See you in a few hours." Delores took Tyler's hand.

"Mr. Aaron, hi and bye." Tyler waved as her brother held the door for them.

"I scored a great sale at Walmart on fabric." Aaron handed her the bag.

Bria pulled out plaid, floral, and cartoon-character cotton fabric. "This should last a while. I'll have time to cut it in neckerchiefs after Brownie. My next appointment isn't until three." Bria folded the fabric and tucked it on a shelf below the counter. "Delores dropped off muffins."

"I got subs." Aaron pulled two from another bag. "Walmart has a Subway."

"Put it in the fridge. I'll eat it later."

"I'll make sure you don't forget. You gotta keep up your strength." Aaron headed to the bathing room. "Hey, Lloyd." He yelled over the sound of running water. "I got lunch. It's in the fridge whenever you're ready." He returned to the front and made fresh coffee.

"What a hypocrite." Bria crossed her arms. "When are you eating?"

"I ate a footlong in the Subway—not covered in dog hair."

"Don't remind me." Bria chuckled.

The doorbell rang again. A huge bouquet of daisies and mums accompanied a delivery man. "Bria Willis?"

She waved.

"Sign here. Have a nice day." The man nodded as he left.

"Marc's got it bad." Aaron elbowed her arm.

Bria moved the flowers to the end of the counter, then removed the card. "Looking forward to Saturday night."

"Ahh, so sweet." Aaron received a swat from her.

"Grow up, big brother." Bria laughed.

"He's a keeper, kid." Aaron grabbed the ringing phone, leaving Bria to bask in the joy of her keeper boyfriend.

She stroked the daisy petals, and the aroma of fresh-cut flowers filled her senses. She hadn't received flowers since high school—a prom corsage. After high school, she was in a relationship with Mitchell. He'd considered flowers lame. Instead, it was extravagant gifts that came with a heavy price tag on her end. Marc was a keeper. But was she? Would he care so much if he knew everything? Could she ever bring the pain close enough to the surface to tell him?

"Ma'am, he's ready for you to work your magic." Lloyd's pronouncement brought Bria's thoughts to the present. This shop, this career, gave her so much joy. She headed to her grooming station as her phone buzzed.

She read the text. "Did you get them?"

"I love them." She texted back.

"Miss you."

What a romantic. He'd texted often with funny emojis and GIFs. Bria chose a GIF of a child clapping her hands and sent it. She didn't have time for a longer text, and Marc made it much too tempting.

Brownie's hair was less tangled, but still a challenge. Bria got into the rhythm of his squirms and finished the haircut before he got too restless. A bright red bandanna with a star in the center completed the groom. She placed him in a crate to wait for Delores and Tyler.

Sitting on a stool at the counter, she ate her six-inch veggie sub and looked through a supply catalog. "Hey, Aaron, there's a sale on shampoo. Come see what you think—maybe try something new for once."

The doorbell tinkled. "I can give you an opinion." The familiar baritone sent a delicious shiver through her. He leaned in and took her hand.

"What a pleasant surprise." Bria smiled and closed the catalog. "Brownie is ready to go."

"Great. Tyler is at soccer practice. I promised to pick up Brownie and bring him to watch." Marc gazed at her. "I've missed you."

"Really?"

Bria stared into his handsome face and recalled her anguish over her unworthiness. A knot formed in her throat as his thumb stroked her knuckles.

"Hey, bro. What's up?" Leave it to Aaron to break the private moment.

"Came to get Brownie."

"I'll get him." Aaron pointed at Bria. "Finish every bite of your sub."

Bria saluted. "Yes, sir."

"Kinda bossy." Marc smiled and pointed at the sub. "I imagine you grab food when you can."

"For sure." She took a bite of her half-eaten sandwich, admiring Marc as she chewed. He wore tailored jeans and a Cub's t-shirt. Her fingers tingled at the thought of running her hand through his curly hair.

"Here's Brownie," Aaron interrupted.

Marc laughed at the bandana. "There's a new sheriff in town." He paid the bill and held Bria's hand for a moment. "See you Saturday." He headed for the door then turned and snapped his finger. "I almost forgot. Wednesday night is the school talent show. You guys want to come? Tyler and Brownie are in it."

Aaron leaned over the appointment screen. "Lloyd showed Tyler a killer trick Brownie already knew."

"Tell him to come too. It's at six. Will you guys be done by then?"

"We'll do our best." Bria smiled. "I'd love to see the talent show."

"Tyler will be stoked if you all can make it. But he'll understand if you can't."

Bria watched through the front window as Marc opened the SUV door for Brownie, who eagerly obeyed. He was so different from his first time at the shop.

That adorable dog had helped her enter a new door, too. So far, dates with Marc were great, yet something nettled in her heart. She dismissed the worry. Marc was a good guy. Good guys didn't hurt and betray. *Right, Lord. Please don't let this turn out bad.*

11

Bria, Lloyd, and Aaron grabbed the last three seats in the back of the auditorium. They'd decided to go back and clean the shop after the show. Seeing Tyler and Brownie perform was too much to resist. The first act had just left the stage. According to the program, Tyler and Brownie were near the end.

After watching a parakeet who flipped over playing cards and an assortment of dancers, musicians, and a six-year-old rapper, it was Tyler's turn. He wore a firefighter costume and Brownie had on a firefighter hat made of paper. Tyler took him through basic commands then shouted. "Fire, Fire." A baby started to cry, while Brownie stopped, dropped and rolled. Tyler shouted "Evacuate." And Brownie crawled off stage. There was a round of applause. Bria couldn't have been prouder if he was her own child.

Aaron whistled and Lloyd hooted, Tyler saw them and waved. The school choir sang a few songs while the judges chose the winners. Bria gripped Aaron's arm as they called the names.

Tyler and Brownie were finalists. When he received the first-place trophy for the best animal act, even Bria whistled. Marc turned from his place in the second row and waved. Bria grinned and waved back as Marc headed backstage, she assumed to get Tyler.

The principal waited for the cheers to die down before he continued. "And now for the overall best act, the prize goes to Tyler Willis and his amazing dog Brownie for teaching us all how to get out of a fire safely." He signaled for Marc to join his son on stage The principal handed him the trophy, and he presented it to Tyler. The two of them were beaming, and Brownie's tongue lolled out in a doggy smile.

Bria and the guys waited for the crowd to clear before they approached. Bria hugged the boy and patted Brownie. "You two were wonderful."

Lloyd scratched Brownie's ears. "Good job, boy." Then he turned to Tyler. "You stole the show."

"Great job, kid." Aaron picked him up and spun him around, making the boy laugh. He set him down and shook Marc's hand. "You've got an awesome son."

"Don't I know it." Marc tousled Tyler's hair. "Now we need to get Brownie home so Grammie can take us out for ice cream."

"You are all welcome to come." Grammie joined the group. "My treat."

"We need to go back and clean the shop." Aaron nodded toward Lloyd. "But Bria is free."

She didn't argue. After all, she'd stayed late plenty of times to clean while he joined his friends. Marc took her hand, sending tingles through her as they headed toward the door. She loved spending time with this family.

Could she open her heart to be part of it? Wait, slow down, take it slow. Things might not even work out. She'd rushed into things with Mitch, trying to erase her grief at the loss of Brittany. Now was her chance to decide for herself whether a man was right for her. She squeezed Marc's hand as he walked her to Grammie's car. She'd ridden with Aaron, and her car remained at the shop. Maybe she could ask Marc to take her to work tomorrow. Was it too soon? They were getting together Saturday. And then there was the Tuesday lesson.

THEY HAD POSTPONED their Saturday date because of Tyler had a nasty ear infection. Marc refused to leave his son's side, which only endeared him more. She'd had an extra-long day on Saturday, and the board of the Bow-Wow Rescue Center had meant early Sunday afternoon. She'd not seen or heard from Marc since he'd canceled. The idea of visiting Tyler had floated around in her head, but her heart had told her to back off and not shove her way into their family.

Today was their final dog training lesson and the most crucial. Would the guys be able to maintain control of Brownie?

"This will be the ultimate test." Marc pointed at Brownie as the doorbell rang for the second time.

"Don't act nervous, he can sense your anxiety." Bria whispered then patted Brownie.

"Dogs have superpowers. Who knew?" Marc chuckled.

Tyler raced ahead of him and threw open the door. "Mallory, you're here." He ran to his dad's cousin and hugged the willowy teen around the waist.

Marc signaled Brownie to heel. "Hey, Mallory." He walked toward her with Brownie at his side.

"Hey, Marcellus."

"Mallory, this is my dog trainer extraordinaire, Bria Willis."

"Cool."

"Nice to meet you." Bria gave her a warm smile. "To clarify, the dog was already trained, I trained the guys."

Marc took her hand. "It took special skills to train us."

Everyone laughed, and Brownie barked. Marc extended his flat hand to the dog, who sighed and remained in place.

"Where's Grammie?" Mallory asked.

"She's in the family room altering your prom dress." Marc said. Bria and Mallory were remarkably similar in appearance. Marc's thoughts turned to the vision of seeing Bria in formal wear. "You two are about the same size," he squeezed Bria's shoulder. "I think it would fit you even."

"Ha." Bria smirked, then turned toward Mallory. "I'd love to see your gown."

"Marcellus, I wanted to thank you for buying my prom ticket. Mom told me."

"Marcellus?' Bria's eyes sparkled.

"All my cousin's still call me that. When I was a child, I insisted on being called by my given name." Marc grinned. "I was named after a hero in a romance novel my mom read when she was pregnant with me. My sister is Marigold Aster after Mom's favorite flowers,"

Bria giggled as she gazed into his eyes. "'Tis truly an odd family."

He kissed her nose, and she leaned into his chest.

Brownie barked, and they followed the sound. Tyler held the treat high. "Sit, stay, play dead." Brownie did everything he asked in quick succession. Tyler rewarded the dog.

"Wow, Ty, your dog is amazing." Mallory petted Brownie. "Grammie, you made that dress look so much better." Mallory hugged her. "Mom found it at a thrift shop, and I was kinda upset about wearing a bargain dress."

Bria fingered the formal satin dress hanging on the open closet door. "It's amazing. I'd wear it in a heartbeat."

"Go try it on in my bedroom." Grammie waved her toward her room.

"Please, I'd love to see how a model looks in it." Mallory held out the dress. "Grammie told me you had been a model. That's so cool!"

Bria didn't seem offended Mallory knew her past. Marc felt the knot in his stomach dissolve.

"It's your dress." Bria kept her arms to her side.

"Please." Mallory pulled out her phone. "I'm going to post the picture for all my friends to see. Wearing a dress a model wore is...awesome"

"I'd love to see you in it." Marc had only seen her in a skirt on their not-a-date date.

"All right. But Mallory you have to post a picture wearing it too."

"Deal." Mallory handed over the dress.

Bria disappeared into the bedroom. She returned with her hair in an updo, adding even more of a fairy-tale image.

"What a great idea, looking for a prom dress at a thrift shop." Bria's words turned to a giggled as she jerked her hand away from Brownie. "Stop it." The canine ceased licking her hand.

Marc signaled heel, and Brownie came to his side. He watched her twirl in the dress, causing his heart to soar.

Brownie woofed. Tyler's eyes shone. "Wow! You're Cinderella."

Bria blushed. "Thanks, kiddo." She turned to Marc.

"You do look like a princess. So beautiful."

"Thank you, Marcellus." She giggled.

"Miss Bria, are you going to prom?" Tyler asked.

"No, honey, I'm too old."

"Is Daddy too old?"

"Absolutely, sport." Marc picked him up and tickled him. Tyler chuckled, then put his small hands on Marc's cheeks.

"Daddy, can't you have your own prom?" Tyler looked between them.

"Proms are for high school kids, Ty, not adults." Mallory's explanation seemed to deflate Tyler.

Mallory snapped a picture, then added. "Now it's my turn."

Bria and Mallory left to change.

Marc sat his son down as the boy sighed. "But I can take Miss Bria to a fancy dinner. She can wear a fancy dress, and I'll wear my black suit."

"Cool. I need to tell Grammie." Tyler's eyes shone. "She can take pictures." He squirmed out of Marc's arms, headed toward the hall, then ran back as Bria returned wearing her casual jeans and yellow tank top. "You got to buy Miss Bria a cor... cor...flower." Then he raced down the hall with Brownie on his heels.

"So, Miss Bria, will you be my prom date?" Marc turned to face her.

"I'm sorry, Tommy already asked me." She leaned into him and caressed his chin.

Marc stared into her joy-filled eyes.

"If you don't mind the commute to Chicago, I know a fantastic restaurant—coincidentally also called The Chicago. When I worked in the city, I took clients there. The food is spectacular."

"I assume I'll need to wear my little black dress." Bria's eyes sparkled.

"Can't wait to see it."

Her lips were so tempting. If not for the potential audience, he'd pull her close and taste them. Instead, he took her hand. But his heart beat against his ribs in anticipation of their first real date.

⁓

BRIA CAPTURED a sigh and patted her upswept hair before ringing Marc's doorbell.

This was it. She was really doing it, a formal date meant more than a coffee with dessert, friends hiking, or spending time with his son as a threesome.

Over the last week, she'd vacillated between going or calling it off. Wearing a dinner dress felt strange—the first time she'd worn one since her modeling days. This time, she dressed for herself. No one would judge her appearance in the public arena. She took a cleansing breath and pressed the doorbell.

Marc looked every bit the catalog model as he opened the door wearing a black suit with a monochromatic blue tie. A delicious shiver went through her as he took in her form with an approving grin. "That little black dress doesn't disappoint."

"It's not too much?" Bria had applied more makeup than usual. She'd went to a salon to get her hair done and wore silver slingbacks with small heels. Marc stepped away from the door to let her inside. Silver hoops dangled from her ears and matched her necklace and bracelets. She carried her black jacket with silver sequins.

"It's perfect." Marc leaned in and whispered, "Got me a really hot prom date."

She giggled and turned her head to receive his kiss. His musky after-shave alluring. "You're not so bad yourself." Her voice was husky.

"Miss Bria, you're the most beautiful woman in the world." Tyler spread his arms wide.

"Thank you." Bria opened her arms, and the boy hugged her gently.

Tyler smiled up at her.

"Miss Bria and I need to leave."

"Wait." Tyler headed to the kitchen. "Grammie, hurry."

"Oh, I almost forgot." Marc handed her a vase of roses. "I thought a corsage was a bit too high-school."

"So, we're not going to prom?" Bria took the vase of red roses and sniffed their fragrance. "So sweet. Can I drop these at home?"

"Sure, we'll stop on our way."

"Stand still." Grammie took several pictures while Tyler told them how to pose.

"We really need to go now, or we'll miss the train." Marc hugged his son.

"We're taking the train?" Bria tried to keep her voice neutral as Marc helped her with her jacket. She hadn't taken the train to Chicago since Brittany's chemo. Bria and her siblings had taken the train to visit every weekend, while her parents' kept vigil at her sister's bedside.

Tyler took her hand. "Daddy promised me he wouldn't drive that far, so I won't worry." Bria could endure the train for this little guy.

"Don't drink and don't say mean things if Daddy makes you mad."

Bria's heart hitched at the serious expression on his face. "I promise."

Marc took her hand. They dashed to the car, delivered her roses, and arrived at the train station with minutes to spare. They settled in their seats.

"I'm glad I wore these shoes," Bria said with a straight face.

"Are you being sarcastic about running in heels?"

"These are not stilettos. I didn't want to make you uncomfortable by wearing heels that made me taller than you."

Marc shook his head. "Wow! Do you think I've got a giant ego?"

She laughed. "According to Aaron, guys don't like their dates to look taller."

"I wouldn't know. I've never dated a woman taller than me." Marc chuckled.

"Most models are closer to six feet. I'm on the short side. When I did run-way work, I had to wear four-inch heels." Why did she feel the need to mention modeling? That was in the past, best forgotten.

"Do you miss it?" Marc's question didn't sting her heart as much. This time it felt more like a get-to-know-you question. No judgment.

Bria ran her thumb over his palm. "Not at all. I prefer dressing up for a date like a normal woman, rather than being pursued by a gang of camera creeps."

"Thanks for dressing up for me."

Marc's sincerity touched a lonely place in her heart. She gave him a quick kiss, then turned to watch the landscape pass by. The comfortable silence between them while they held hands felt right. Passengers flowed in and out as the train stopped at depots along the route.

Bria's thoughts dwelled on Tyler's request. "Why is Tyler so worried about you driving to Chicago?"

"He was in the car when his mother crashed into another car. She'd been drinking."

"Of course, you told me. Now I understand the drinking comment. But why'd he think I'd get mad at you?"

"The day of the accident, his mother packed the car. She wrestled our son into his car seat. He made a scene, begging her to not leave me." Marc turned his face, before Bria noticed moisture dampened his eyes. "Tyler had screamed he didn't want to go moments before she died."

"Poor baby." Bria searched her handbag for a tissue and dabbed her eyes. "I imagine if we stay out too late, he'll worry."

Marc drew a breath. "I'm hoping he'll go to bed instead."

"If you need to call and check in, I understand. We can make it an early evening."

He squeezed her hand. "You're awesome." Cuddling close, she felt the tension leave him. "Hope you love the restaurant."

"Good company makes all the difference."

Marc laughed until tears streaked his face. A man at a nearby table scowled at him. Bria's family stories made for dangerous dinner conversation. He cut his steak into small pieces to avoid a possible choking hazard when bouts of laughing came.

"Stop." Marc took a sip of water.

"I'm sorry. I suppose laughing like hyenas is too out of place here." Bria wiggled her eyebrows. "Shall we talk about the stock market?"

"I know nothing about that." Marc exhaled and took another sip of water. "We could discuss the celebrity who arrived when we did." He looked toward the tall ivory double doors to the private dining room. "Did you notice all the paparazzi hanging around?" Marc stared into her eyes. "Must've been tough dealing with all the photographers."

"You have no idea." She smoothed the linen napkin in her lap and gave him a nervous smile. "Can we not talk about my past?"

Marc took another bit of steak just as the celebrity, dripping in bling, and his entourage headed toward the exit. Photo flashes filled the room. Diners took pictures with their cell phones. The celebrity made a beeline out of the restaurant, and the room became silent again. Bria's pleasant disposition morphed into sadness. Marc reached across the table and laid his hand atop hers. "We could talk about the latest Avenger movie."

She sighed, slipped her hand from his, and picked up her fork. "I've never seen them." Bria cut a small slice of her rainbow trout. "My job can leave me exhausted. All I want to do when I get home is sleep."

"What's your favorite movie?" Marc refused to let any silence fall between them until he brightened her mood.

"I love the BBC versions of the classics— Jane Eyre, Sense and Sensibility, Pride and Prejudice. Often I fall asleep part way through a Hallmark movie."

Marc's phone chimed. "It's Tyler. He wants to know if we're having a good time." He took a few moments to take pictures of the tall, arched ceiling and the other diners sitting in upholstered chairs with linen tablecloths. Then he pulled Bria close and took a selfie. "Tyler will love seeing where we are." Marc added a text with the photos and read it to Bria. "Having a blast. Time for you to be in bed."

The phone dinged again. "Tyler asked, 'how come no balloons?'"

"He's a great speller for five." Bria took his phone and texted, "We miss the balloons too. Have sweet dreams."

"Perfect." Marc slid his cell back into his jacket pocket. "Grammie showed Tyler how to voice to text."

"That explains the perfect spelling." Bria's smile returned. "Do we have time for dessert?"

"Absolutely." Marc pushed his empty plate to the side and signaled for the waiter. "Dessert."

"Can I interest you in a double chocolate layer cake?" The waiter rattled off several other choices.

"They all sound wonderful." Bria's cute look of indecision with her left eyebrow posed ever so slightly gave Marc an idea.

"Is it possible to get a sample plate?"

"Let me see what I can do." The waiter moved toward the kitchen.

Bria leaned forward. The gentle scent of cologne lingered between them. "Truth is, I haven't eaten dessert in seven years until our non-date."

"What?"

"I was on a very strict diet as a model. Desserts were forbidden." Bria nodded. "I got out of the habit of eating sweets. Aaron tempts me occasionally with a granola bar when I'm starving."

The waiter arrived with tiny slices and squares of the various treats. "Looks awesome. Thanks. Refills on our coffee, please." He turned to Bria. "The Dessert Nazis aren't here. So, enjoy tasting all this deliciousness."

Marc forked a piece of chocolate cake and offered it to her, and she pulled the morsel from the fork with her lips. Her tongue retrieved a stray bit of frosting from the corner of her mouth. Oh, if she only knew how that simple action affected him. The delight in her eyes as she savored the treat made the price tag of this evening worth it.

Bria took off her heels and leaned on Marc's shoulder as the train pulled out of Union Station. "My feet aren't accustomed anymore to wearing heels for more than an hour."

"If it makes you feel better...." Marc leaned forward, untied his dress shoes, and set them to the side. "Ahh, my blisters, thank me." He pulled her to him. "You are so laid back. Just what I need." His phone buzzed in his pocket. Marc disengaged himself from her and checked it. "Grammie says Tyler went to sleep and to take our time coming home."

"That's nice. But tomorrow has a full schedule." Bria took his hand. "This has been so much fun. Thank you for this special night."

Marc pulled her to him and kissed her forehead. "I so needed tonight out. Thank you for agreeing to Tyler's suggestion and dressing so...." His voice deepened. She slapped his arm. They chuckled and snuggled close.

Bria relished the security of resting in his arms. Maybe Aaron was right. This guy was amazing. If she had a check list he would check all the boxes. She brushed a loose hair off his face and burrowed closer, the rhythm of the train and the warmth of his body peaceful.

"Bria." Her name came through a fog. "Bria, it's our stop."

She jerked awake. "Why did you let me sleep?"

"I enjoyed being your pillow." Marc rose and extended his hand. He'd replaced his shoes while she'd slept. She slipped on her heels and took his hand.

The moon gleamed high in the night sky, and they could see a few stars sparkled above the city lights.

"Let's do this again."

"Go to Chicago on the train?" Bria pulled her purse strap over her shoulder.

"Another date. Something more casual." Marc placed his hand on the small of her back and escorted her from the train.

"Sure, when?" Bria slipped her hand into his as they strolled to Marc's car.

"In a few weeks. I know how that sounds." Marc shook his head. "I've got two projects back-to-back that I need to complete. Knowing I have a date to look forward to will keep me on task." He kissed her hand before opening her door.

"I understand. I've plenty to keep me distracted until then." Bria appreciated his honesty. Waiting two weeks gave her time to evaluate their growing relationship. She'd rushed into the last one.

Not making that mistake again.

12

A week later, Bria stood in line with her grocery cart. She checked its contents against her list. Aaron let her leave early, only because she agreed to do the shopping for this Sunday's family barbeque. Aaron had invited Marc and Tyler. Extra time with Marc brought a smile. Tyler could even bring Brownie.

She glanced at the nearby magazine rack. Her heart chilled.

She grabbed a copy of *The Scoop* and stared at the cover. Anger bubbled inside. The headline read *Super Model Out of Hiding with New Love. Mitchell Treat Heartbroken.* An inset, cropped photo of Mitchell, grief-stricken at his mother's funeral, appeared in the photo's corner of Bria and Marc. She hated seeing her face on that rag again. A knot formed in her stomach.

She glared at the photo as if she had the superpower to set the paper on fire. Rage seared through her as she tossed it into her cart. While the cashier finished bagging her items, she texted Marc. "Are you home? You need to see something."

"Will be soon. Sounds serious."

"I'll stop by later." Her hands shook as she paid for her purchases. The car clock indicated it was past time for the shop to be closed. She texted her brother 911 before she headed home.Her brother had been her rock when the paparazzi hounded her when she'd walked away from modeling. He'd help them sort out this invasion of her privacy.

~

SHE UNLOADED groceries with shaky hands. She should never have gone to Chicago. Who knew there'd be a celebrity and a swarm of paparazzi there?

The temptation to throw the milk in her refrigerator to release frustration died with the thought of cleaning up the mess. Her phone dinged. Marc. "I'll be home in five." She grabbed the paper, calming at the vision of commiserating with Marc.

Bria speed-walked toward Marc's house. A brand-new, red Mustang rumbled by and pulled into Delores's driveway.

Marc exited from the driver's side.

How in the world...? Bria's blood ran cold. Covering her mouth, she froze in place on the sidewalk. *Marc must have leaked where we'd be on our date. That's how the paparazzi knew where I was.... Obviously, they rewarded him in full.*

Her anger erupted at the sight of Marc's betrayal.

~

MARC EXITED Grammie's new Mustang. He had to admit, driving it brought back fond memories of his grandfather. They'd dropped off his SUV for service. He held out the keys to Grammie once she'd exited the passenger seat.

"Thanks for letting me take it for a spin."

She laid a hand on his arm. "I'm glad you enjoyed it. The pleasure was all mine."

He helped Tyler out of the backseat. "Go let Brownie out."

Marc checked his phone. Bria's "on my way" text brought a smile. He went to the bathroom and ran a comb through his hair. He grabbed a Life Saver mint from the bowl on the end table as the doorbell rang.

Bria stood on the porch with fire in her eyes.

"Hey, you okay?"

"Now I get it." Angry tears spilled down her cheeks.

She threw a newspaper against his chest. He retrieved it from the floor. "What's this about?" Marc stared at the headline. "Wow.... This is messed up."

"Is it?" Her glare stabbed at his integrity. "I wondered how that photographer knew who I was." Her voice choked. "Then I saw the shiny new Mustang convertible in the driveway."

"What?" Marc stared at her furious face in confusion. What are you talking about?"

"You went on and on about getting another one if you had the money...apparently you do now." She pushed a hair out of her moisture-filled eyes. "I was so wrong about you." Arms crossed, she stared at the ground, her voice a whisper. "What a fool I've been." Anger rimmed her eyes as she glared at him. "Wiggling into my affection with all your kind words and kisses, so you could collect the big payday. I don't ever..." She stormed out.

Marc stood in the open doorway, feeling like his world had just imploded. He shut the door, numb.

Grammie came from the kitchen after the door slammed. "Dear, what was that all about?"

Tyler stood at the front window with Brownie at his side, then turned and scowled at Marc. "Why'd you make Miss Bria mad?"

"Hold on here." Marc ran his fingers through his hair. "I did nothing. She was mad when she arrived."

He reached to hug Tyler.

His son stepped away. "You better say sorry."

"It's a misunderstanding, sport. I'm not sure what's going on."

"You made her cry." Tyler yelled. "I saw her walking home crying." He ran from the room.

"Tyler!"

Grammie sat on the couch and patted the place next to her. "Give him a minute. Tell me what happened."

A loud knock at the front door brought Marc to his feet. "I'll get it."

Marc opened it to find Aaron's raised fist.

"Before I punch you in the face, tell me your side of the story."

Marc stepped aside for him to enter. "Well, this day just keeps getting better."

Aaron shook his head and snorted. "Tell me about it. She's a puddle of tears and mad at you." He strode in. "Hello, Delores." Aaron sat on the edge of the chair across from the sofa, returning his attention to Marc. "Bro, what did you do?"

"Honestly, I don't understand any of this. Earlier, Bria texted me saying she needed to show me something. She came over with her claws out and threw this at me." Marc showed him the paper. "She screamed about Grammie's car and left."

"Delores, that's *your* new car?" Aaron laughed and shook his head.

"Yes, my pink baby was twenty years old. I needed a new ride. My late husband always loved Mustangs—so why not get one?" Grammie said.

"She thought the Mustang was mine." Marc rubbed his temples. "I should have put that together. I've never seen the angry side of her before." Marc hoped to never see it again. "Why would she assume I'd set her up?" It hurt to know she'd jump to the dark side so fast.

Aaron sighed. "Bria got hurt bad by crazy tabloid photographers and her ex-boyfriend. One guy noticed her at a fund-raiser for Habitat for Humanity and started stalking her. It got real ugly. Her lawyer got a restraining order. Paparazzi give her panic attacks." Aaron's hands fisted as he talked. "Today, this photo brought back bad memories." Aaron took a breath and squinted. "Then she saw Delores' car, and the tornado touched down."

"Let me talk to her." Marc headed for the door. "I'll straighten this out." *Father, give me the right words.* The wrong words could ruin what they had, and Tyler would be hurt again.

∼

BRIA OPENED the door to Tyler's tear-streaked face. He held out a handful of dandelions. "Don't be mad. Daddy's sorry. Whatever he did he won't do it again. I promise."

"Tyler." Bria squatted next to him. "You can't fix what your daddy did." She hugged him. "It's not your fault."

"Please don't stay mad." The boy's sorrow-filled eyes almost melted her resolve. Maybe she wouldn't press charges against Marc.

"Tyler, go home." She stood up and pointed to the door.

"Please, don't stay mad." Wrapping his arms around her waist made his plea more insistent. Bria's heart broke at the anxiety in his face.

"Tyler, this is a grown-up problem. You have to let the grown-ups work it out." She hugged him again. He clung to her, crying. She pushed him away and turned him toward the door. "Go home, sweetie." She text Delores that she'd sent him home. A thumbs up emoji let her know Delores would be watching. She couldn't go back up the block.

∼

MARC LED Aaron to Bria's. They met a tearful Tyler on the sidewalk.

"Son, you can't run off without telling me."

"I told her you're sorry, Daddy. But she didn't believe me."

Marc pulled Tyler into a hug. "Go on home" He looked toward the house where Grammie stood on the porch. Miss Bria and I need to talk."

"Okay, but don't yell." Tyler's lips shaped a scolding pout.

"I won't. I promise. Tell Grammie I said to give you a snack." Marc watched as his son plodded home, Tyler's shoulders sagging. Once Tyler was inside, they continued walking.

Aaron cupped Marc's shoulder. "That's rough. I'll be your wingman. Bria can be irrational when she's upset."

"Thanks. I can handle this myself."

Marc followed Aaron into Bria's living room. He took a deep breath to gain composure. "Bria, it's not what you think."

She glowered at him.

"It's not, sis." Aaron stretched his hands out, palms facing the ground. "Calm down and listen."

Bria scowled at her brother. If looks killed, the big guy would be down for the count. Wow! Janet had gone off over nothing. This Bria made his heart clinch. He couldn't help comparing the two. He'd developed the habit of shutting down when his ex got like this. Not this time.

BRIA FOUGHT MORE tears as she maintained her sour expression. *How can Aaron take his side?*

"I'm leaving now." Aaron pulled his keys from his pocket and kissed Bria on the cheek. She shrugged away and crossed her arms. Aaron shut the door without looking back. Bria stared out the picture window, feeling trapped in a betrayal that cut deep. She turned to face her adversary.

"Please, let me explain." Marc's hurt expression contradicted her mind's traitor image.

"Fine." Bria sat back in the overstuffed chair. Marc perched on the edge of the sofa.

"The new car belongs to Grammie. She bought it yesterday. My SUV is in the shop today."

"Delores bought a Mustang?" How out of character for the older woman.

"She needed a new car, and my grandfather loved Mustangs. Grammie misses him, and the Mustang makes her happy. She says it'll keep her young."

Bria released a long sigh. She slipped her shaking hands between the chair cushion and armrests. "Okay."

"Are you still mad at me?" Concern edged Marc's blue eyes.

"No." She shivered, releasing some of her angst. "But I'm still upset."

He leaned forward to touch her.

"Don't." She pressed her body into the far corner of her chair. "I need space. I need to process."

"All right." Marc wiped his hands on his jeans. Silence covered their awkwardness for several minutes. "How can I help you process?"

"Be honest." Bria looked into his eyes, searching for any hint of falsehood. "Did you know any of those photographers? Did you know they would be there?"

"How would I know any paparazzi?" Marc's jaw tightened with the question. "I know what it's like to be hounded. When Janet died, the accident was all over the news. Reporters wanted to interview Ty. I worked for a high-profile company that already had some bad press the week before. I was just another piece of shark bait for the media."

Marc leaned forward. "Bria, I took you there because I wanted to give you a special night. If I had known that rapper dude was going to be there, I'd have picked another restaurant." He ran his hands through his hair. "There were flashes going off all over the room when that guy's entourage walked out the door. One photographer may have recognized you."

"I didn't notice. I was too busy trying to blend in with the other diners." She rose from her chair, putting distance between them. "It makes sense. I'm sorry."

He nodded, still giving her his full attention. Bria relaxed but kept her distance. "This whole thing brings back memories I've worked hard to forget." She hated the hitch in her voice.

"I have an idea." Marc looked about the room. "I handed the paper to Aaron. Did he take it with him?"

"No. Why?" Bria stepped to the kitchen counter to retrieve the paper. He joined her.

"Look here." Marc pointed to the photo credit. "Darien Richards."

"Darien?" Her heart sank. "He stalked me for weeks after I broke up with Mitchell Treat and left the agency for good."

Bria crossed her arms. I can't believe after five years anyone cares about a retired model. She picked up the paper and turned the page toward him. "It went viral all over social media." Bria threw the paper in the trash.

"No wonder you're mad." Marc's voice held a low growl. "If I'd noticed the photographer I'd have smashed his camera.

Marc ran his hand down her arm. The fire she felt from his touch brought fearful reminders of Mitch's hands on her overshadowing Marc's tenderness. She pulled away, straightened and stepped behind the counter, creating more of a barrier between them.

"Are you going to call that photographer?" His question sounding more like a command.

"No." Bria paced the room. "He's probably gotten all the mileage he can get out of that one photo. I'll have my lawyer send him a letter reminding him to stay away."

"What will you do if he comes around?" He stood beside her. She moved toward the counter again.

"I'll sic Bruno or Charlotte on him. Bruno's bark brings terror to the heart of all who hear it. Charlotte is a yelpy fox terrier who loves to bite."

"Sounds like a plan." Marc laughed. "Are we good?"

"I think so." But Bria couldn't bury the freshly dug up.

"We still on for Saturday?"

She'd forgotten in her emotional meltdown that Aaron had suggested she invite his family to her parent's farm. She couldn't very well uninvite them. And she was ashamed at how easily her mistrust came to the surface when she saw the car. Another mark against her ability to have a relationship.

"Yes." Bria opened the door. She needed time to get out of her own head. Marc's resolute nod formed a lump in her throat.

"Call me?"

"Sure." Bria wanted to fling herself into his arms and let the warmth of his presence soothe all the wounded places. Instead, she watched him close the door.

13

"**D**addy, I'm stuck." Tyler squirmed in his car seat.

Marc opened the back door of Grammie's convertible to unfasten his son's twisted seatbelt. Tyler's excitement made the task a challenge. Marc pushed his son's hands away a few times before he finally got the job done. The twisted knot in his stomach wasn't as easy to untangle.

Brownie climbed out. The two ran up the driveway toward the Willis's house.

Marc had called Aaron to get his take on the wisdom of coming. He'd assured him it would be fine, but it was up to him. Would Bria be welcoming? Surely Tyler and Grammie would be a good buffer if she was still upset over the photo. A photo that wasn't his fault. He sighed as he closed the car door. Her few brief texts since the misunderstanding confounded him. Where did their relationship stand?

Grammie laid a hand on his arm. "It'll be all right. Bria didn't say not to come."

Marc smiled at Grammie. "You read my mind." Funny how she always knew when he was troubled.

She clicked the key fob and the trunk opened. "Get out the picnic basket for me."

The Willis farm's long, winding driveway led to a brick ranch with a few outbuildings. The yard boasted several lush flower beds in a variety of colors. Marc followed Grammie to a gazebo just past the garage. Inside had been placed a food table to the left of the grill, onto which Aaron flopped two porterhouse steaks. The aroma of beef searing made Marc's mouth water.

"How do you like yours?" Aaron set down the spatula and shook Marc's hand.

"Medium rare." Marc grabbed a soda from a cooler nearby and sat at the picnic table.

"Coming up." Aaron nodded toward the food table. "Mom and Dad are bringing the rest of the food out in a few minutes."

"Where's Bria?" Marc hoped he sounded casual.

"Helping mom." Aaron flipped the steak and glanced up. "There she is."

Bria wore jeans and a pink checkered blouse with her hair in a ponytail. The country-girl look suited her. Nervous sweat dotted his forehead, and he wiped it with his arm. Bria held two covered dishes. Marc jogged over and grabbed one. "Let me help."

"Thanks." Bria's smile was subdued. She paused. "Where is Tyler?" She looked around. "Ah, he found Sky and Logan."

Marc chuckled as Tyler tried to carry two oversized cats at once. They yowled and shot out of his arms. Tyler appeared unconcerned and ran toward Brownie.

"Those old barn cats are not people-pets." Bria chuckled. Her laughter relaxed Marc a bit.

The screen door opened behind her. An older couple headed their way.

"This is my dad, John Willis."

A graying version of Aaron without tats nodded toward him. "My hands are full, or I'd shake yours. Good to meet you."

"This is my mom." A gentle breeze blew hair in Bria's face, and she pushed the strays from her forehead. "Debbie."

Debbie handed her dish to Bria and surprised Marc with a hug. "Welcome to our home. Bria and Aaron have told me nice things about you."

She stepped back and gave him the same brilliant smile Bria shared when she was happy. "Delores, so glad you could make it." She hugged his grandmother.

Grammie held Debbie's elbows. "So good to see you again."

"How do you know each other?" Marc looked between his grandmother and Debbie.

"Delores and I volunteer at the food pantry." Debbie gave Grammie a shoulder hug. "She and my mom were best friends as children. My folks moved to Florida years ago. When Mom passed two years ago, then Delores and I reconnected."

Marc sensed their closeness. It was just like Grammie to mother whoever needed it.

Bria walked ahead of them to the gazebo. Marc's eyes strayed from watching her hips sway to Brownie, who gave a joyful bark when three big dogs approached him. Marc had no idea what breeds they were, but their deep-throated barks sent a shiver through him.

Aaron whistled from his place at the grill. The trio sat. Brownie followed suit. Marc shook his head in amazement, his stomach unknotting. Tyler patted each dog in turn. Aaron whistled again and signaled. All four dogs came to him. He gave them each a morsel of steak, then they trotted over to rest in the shade of a large maple tree. Marc and Tyler joined the others under the gazebo.

"Nice ride." John glanced over at the convertible.

"Want to test drive it?' Grammie held out the key fob.

"I'll take you up on that later." John smiled as he poured iced tea from a large glass canaster.

Tyler took his dad's hand. "When do we eat?"

Bria reached out her arms, and Tyler went in for a hug. "I want you to meet my parents. Mr. And Mrs. Willis."

"You have a mommy and a daddy? Why don't you live with them?" Tyler's question made them laugh.

"Because I'm a grown-up." Bria ruffled his hair.

Tyler looked over at Aaron. "Where do you live?"

"Here." Aaron flipped a few burgers.

"You look all grown up to me."

Aaron laughed. "Looks can be deceiving."

"You got that right." John shoulder-bumped his son away from the grill. "Let a grown up show you how to grill. Tyler, would you like a hamburger?"

"Sure."

Tyler peppered Mr. Willis with questions. The dogs had wandered back to the gazebo and took a sitting stance behind Aaron. The largest one whined. Brownie sniffed the air with his tongue hanging out, appearing to wait for some tidbit to fall to the floor. Aaron gave each of the dogs a large bowl of kibble with bits of meat. They gobbled them up and went back to their place at the tree. Brownie followed them.

"This place is great." Marc sat beside Bria in a patio chair.

"I love coming out here in the summer. I'll sit on the porch glider and read." Bria's smile didn't reach her eyes.

The meal was served, and Tyler ate just enough to be excused. He and Brownie played catch and raced each other and Aaron's three mongrels.

"Hey, Tyler, I got a frisbee." Aaron jogged over to Marc's son and the dogs.

"Do you want to come, Daddy?" Tyler raced toward Aaron.

"Nah, have fun." He watched Aaron throw the frisbee for the dogs. They waited as he called their names. Each dog took a turn. The grace with which the canines retrieved the disc impressed him. Brownie interrupted the order by chasing the frisbee at the same time. The other dogs always managed to beat him. Soon he caught on to the game when Aaron called his name. Tyler cheered them on and took turns throwing the disc. His son's frisbee technique left much to be desired. The dogs often trotted after the frisbee and retrieved it from the ground. Neither Aaron nor the dogs complained. He made a mental note to buy a frisbee and teach Tyler how to throw it properly.

Marc enjoyed the hospitality of the Willis's. Bria chatted with Grammie and her parents, but said little to him. Aaron had extended the invitation. Did Bria wish he hadn't come? He couldn't leave too early. Tyler would make a fuss, and he didn't want to ruin Grammie's visit either. Besides, Marc needed to know where he stood with Bria.

John leaned forward and gripped the arms of his chair. "Delores, let's see that new hotrod of yours."

Laughter trailed in the direction of the convertible as John and Debbie chatted with Grammie. John sat in the driver's seat with the door open. *What great people.*

Janet's parents had big dreams for their daughter. He hadn't been in them. Even now, her parents rarely visited. They'd send expensive gifts to Tyler and had set up a college fund. Tyler stopped asking when they were coming. Grammie did her best to fill the hurt places. It was obvious Tyler had attached himself to this family. *God don't let him get hurt again.*

"Marc?" Bria came outside after putting away the food. "Want to go for a walk?"

He reached for her hand, and she didn't resist. Marc smiled at the feeling of her hand in his. "I need a walk after all that delicious food."

"There's a path through the woods behind the house that leads to the creek." She led him toward the woods. "My great-great-great grandparents built a log cabin near the creek. It's gone now. Aaron built a bench in high school from the wood. It sits on the spot where the cabin was."

"It must be great to have roots like that. My parents moved a lot." Even Grammie and Grandpa were transplants. "Do you guys go in for genealogies?"

"My mom is big on it. She printed off our family tree and taped it together. It filled one whole wall in our living room. That was when I was ten. Lots of married cousins and their kids have been added."

Two finches flew past them toward the nest they were building in a nearby tree. Squirrels chittered as they chased each other. Nature was building families as he walked holding hands with the most awesome woman he'd ever met. Could they build a future together?

Bria squeezed his hand. "You okay?"

"Yeah. Nature walks make me contemplative." Marc grinned, the action lifting his spirit. "Much more relaxing than hiking over Deadman's Rock."

Bria giggled. "I'll race you to the bench." She ran before Marc could see where she pointed. He caught up with her and grabbed her hand. They slowed and strolled to the bench.

"Wow, he did a great job." Marc stroked the bench, admiring the filigree trim. "Nothing like any woodworking project I would have done in high school."

"Aaron talked a woodcarver into teaching him when he was twelve. He's built several pieces of furniture for my parents."

"Why didn't he go into that business?"

"He might, someday."

"Why dog grooming?"

"He worked his way through college as a dog washer and walker. He bought out his boss and took classes."

BRIA KNEW the small talk couldn't last forever. Marc needed an answer. They sat on the bench. The scent of his body wash and barbeque smoke drifted her way as she tried to keep a bit of distance between them on the bench. "Did you ever want to do something different than web designs?" She picked up a rock resting at her feet and waited for his answer.

"I thought I wanted my own advertising company. I'd majored in marketing and business in college. When I finally got a job in advertising, it was too cut-throat. I don't miss it. Now my whole focus is Tyler's happiness. Web designing and building marketing plans for small businesses helps me provide for my son. Working from home gives me flexible hours I can devote to Tyler."

Marc leaned forward and folded his hands in front of him gazing at the water then straightened and turned to look at her. He searched her face. A lump formed in her throat and the urge to kiss him wrestled with her common sense. She waited as he cleared his throat.

"Bria, I need to know if you plan to keep on being a part of Tyler's happiness." The longing in his eyes ripped at her heart. "And if I'm a part of your happiness."

Bria rose and walked toward the creek. Two mallards swam by, the male duck pursuing the female. As the male got close the female went airborne. He followed as she landed on the other side of the creek where another male joined the two. The second male chased the first away and the female followed him. They waddled off together. The first male paddled away quacking.

Marc stood beside her. "Are you breaking up with me?"

"No."

"Then why the cold breeze between us?" Marc pulled her into a side hug. "Be honest."

The pressure on her shoulder told her how vulnerable he'd made himself. She pulled away and stared at the creek.

"I'm confused."

"About us?"

She rubbed her lips together. "About who I am anymore. Mitch turned me into something I came to hate. My family and my faith have helped me come back to a better version of myself. But I'm still not sure what the final version will look like." She pitched her rock in the creek. It sank to the bottom. *Was it a sign?*

She turned to face him. "I've found my peace working with dogs. Aaron and my folks helped me realize I didn't have to follow Brittany's dreams. The guilt of God allowing my twin, who had so much potential, to get cancer and die devastated me. It seemed so wrong. After all, I was the less gifted one. I foolishly thought I had to become her so her dreams could come true. Brittany was my best friend, I idolized her. I even used her name for my career." Bria sat back on the bench. A robin's song echoed through the branches overhead as Marc sat next to her.

"You're awesome just like you are. Why'd you imitate Brittany?"

"Because I was an immature teen, and when my idol died, I needed to identify with her to find my purpose." Bria put up her hand. "I know—but at the time, it made sense to me." She took a cleansing breath, and Marc squeezed her hand. "I need more time to process my feelings. I jumped into a relationship with Mitch out of grief. I'm not ready to jump into another one out of loneliness." Bria's smile belied her sadness. "I love Tyler, he's a wonderful boy. I want him in my life."

"But not me?" The pain in his voice made her feel like one of the mean girls she'd barely tolerated in high school. They manipulated the other students to made them feel special, then humiliated them when their usefulness was over. How could she fix this without committing to something she wasn't ready for?

"I didn't say that. Friendship I can work with and not hurt Tyler. More than that, I'm not sure." Bria squeezed his hand and released it, feeling like someone cut the lines on the bridge that had taken her from her old life to her new one. "Can we be friends?"

~

FOR TYLER'S SAKE, Marc buried his disappointment and confusion and smiled at this woman he was falling in love with. "Sure. Friendship works for me." *Liar!* He smiled down at her. "You can spend time with Tyler whenever you want."

"Sorry." Her whispered apology did little to salve his wound.

"Hey, you're honest. I respect that." Even in his pain, he could add another item to the pro-side of his list to like—to love—Bria. His throat burned with the unspoken confession.

They walked back to the others. After another hour in which he and Bria attempted more small talk, he called Tyler. "We need to get home."

"I don't want to go." Tyler dragged out the last word. He crossed his arms and glared. "Brownie don't want to leave his new friends."

Grammie rescued Marc from the upcoming tantrum. "Well, young man, it's not all about you. I'm tired and need my rest." She hugged the Willis family and picked up her picnic basket, while Marc scooped up a protesting Tyler.

"Wait. I need to hug everyone goodbye." Tyler cupped Marc's face to be sure he was heard.

Marc let him down and Tyler hugged everyone, including the dogs.

Then he secured him in his car seat, and Grammie drove home. All traces of fatigue faded from Grammie's face as they headed for home. Marc saw Tyler's head sag to the side as he slept. "Thanks."

"For what?" Grammie glanced sideways at him.

"Supporting my decision to go home."

"No problem." She nodded his way and then focused on the road. "Hey, what happened between you and Bria?" Grammie sped up as they moved off the country road to the highway. Marc shared his conversation with Bria, feeling the tension in his shoulders leave when he'd finished.

"Honey, she's not rejecting you. She's trying to be sure of herself. Her parents shared with me some of the details of her former life. It wasn't pretty. Have you told her how Janet was with Tyler?"

"Bits and pieces."

"Do you know anything about Bria's past?"

"A little.... I figured if she wanted me to know, she'd tell me."

"There were things it took twenty years for your grandfather to tell me. He got drafted and served in Vietnam when he was only eighteen. It took decades before he could talk about it. Bria may never tell you of her pain. But her life story is online. At least the bare bones."

"You think I should check out her past?" Marc's jaw tightened.

"Marcellus Antonious Graham, we live in the twenty-first century. Everyone has social media, everyone Googles everyone else. Knowing details from her past could help you understand why she said what she said." Before Marc could mount a defense, she added, "Friends help friends."

Grammie said no more, and they rode home in silence. Could he help Bria? The better question was, should he deep dive into her past? Would it change how he felt about the Bria of the present?

14

Bria, with help from Lloyd, finished grooming Arnold, the possum dog—a Mini Pin and Shih Tzu mix. He laid on her grooming table, acting dead. "Thanks for helping me."

The dog washer chuckled and shook his head.

Bria waited for Lloyd to straighten the dog's limp form.

"Oddest thing I've ever seen." Lloyd shook his head and adjusted Arnold's leg.

"It stopped being funny two years ago." She shaved his matted hair. "Arnold, you faker, I'm almost done."

"What a weird dog." Lloyd held the dog so Bria could shave under his leg.

"He likes baths, but he hates haircuts." Bria chuckled. "You got him dry even though he tried to attack the hair dryer."

"I turned on the dryer in the crate instead." Lloyd had caught on to his job and was fast on his way to learning the skills needed to be a groomer.

"Watch this." Bria finished trimming Arnold's nails. "We're done now."

Arnold hopped up and licked her face. "You want a treat?" She pulled one from the jar on the table nearby. "I'm glad you're not a Great Dane." She tied a green plaid bandana around his neck and handed him to Lloyd. "Put him in a crate. I'll call his mom."

Bria went to the front desk and called Arnold's owner. Aaron collected the payment from a Maltese's dad. The doorbell tinkled as the dog and master left. Aaron stared at her.

"Didn't sleep, did you?"

"What makes you say that?" As if the dark circles under her eyes didn't attest to the fact.

"Come on, I can read you like those mystery novels you love." Aaron hugged her close. "Call him."

She shook her head and pulled away. "I won't do it."

"You got that right. You pushed away a great guy. He's kind, caring, and super-cute."

"You sound like a teenage girl." Bria rearranged the dog toys in the basket on the counter.

"I'm quoting you. Remember, I read your diary when you were fourteen." Aaron laughed when she took a swing. Things had been simpler at fourteen. Her sister had been alive. They'd been innocent of the harsh realities of life.

"Marc and Tyler make you better. I see it. He's good for you. You're good for him."

"I'm not. When I thought he'd used me, I went after him like Mrs. Perkin's Yorkie when you take her toy away. My trust alarms went off."

"Understandable. I think Marc gets it. Couples have misunderstandings all the time." Aaron put his arm around her shoulder again. "Why throw away happiness over this?"

"Well, Mr. Matchmaker," Bria shrugged off his arm and faced him, "tell me why you threw Rachel to the curb. Didn't you say she was the one?"

"Seriously, that was high school." Aaron crossed his arms. "The truth is she dumped me. Said I was dumb as a rock. She wanted more than I could offer." Aaron answered the ringing phone. Bria began straightening the product shelves. How could the woman he'd hoped to marry be so cruel? He'd pretended her move across the country for college was no big thing. "Exploring other options" had been his explanation.

The call ended.

"Is that why you went to college?"

"Yeah." Aaron laughed. "Who knew proving I didn't live in a gravel pit would help me find myself?"

"At least you followed your own dream, not someone else's." Bria pulled the Windex from under the counter and a roll of paper towels. "I wasted years fulfilling Brittany's." She scrubbed off dog-nose prints from the front of the glass display case.

"It was sheer determination. I wanted to see Rachel at the ten-year class reunion and say, 'Ha! Dumb guy got a business degree.'"

"Did you?"

"I won that big trophy the day of the reunion." Aaron pointed to the two-foot high first place nationals grooming trophy. "Proving anything to her didn't matter anymore. You know she friended me on Facebook?"

"Really?" Bria had blocked her old boyfriend on all social media. She rubbed the last nose print off of the glass case.

"She married a neuro-surgeon and has three kids." Aaron answered another call.

Had Bria proven to herself that she was worthy yet? Had her stupid mistakes from the past washed into the sea of forgetfulness?

The phone call ended, and she put the Windex away.

"Trust. That's it...and fear." Bria pulled the hair band off her ponytail and redid it. "I took a giant step back into friendship mode. It's safer."

"No big newsflash there." Aaron wiggled the mouse and typed in an appointment. "Marc could help you learn to trust if you let him."

"Geesh, you're worse than Chloe and Mom put together." Bria kissed Aaron's cheek. "Thanks for caring. But I need to work this out myself." She patted his arm. "And you need to get your own love life."

The doorbell rang, announcing the end to their conversation, but, her brother was like a dog with a new bone. He'd keep at it until every bit of her love life was worked out.

MARC'S EYES blurred from hours of surfing the internet. When he'd tried to find Bria Willis, he'd only found the Doggie Designer Duo's website and other social media. There wasn't much on her before they opened the shop. Deeper digging found a few old articles about Bria winning volunteer of the year for her work at the animal shelter.

Marc warmed his coffee cup in the microwave he kept in his office. "Didn't she say she used her sister's name as a model?"

His search of Brittany Willis exploded with hundreds of links. He gleaned through the photos and articles following her career. The older ones proclaimed she was the next Heidi Klum, and a few mentioned she was being considered for movie roles. "Wow." Marc swallowed the last of his coffee and continued reading.

Besides the viral photo at the restaurant, the most recent posts were five years old. His stomach knotted at seeing pictures of her on the arm of her agent, Mitchell Treat. Lots of partying and celebrity red-carpet events. Marc's heart turned to ice when he found a police report. Bria had been arrested for a DUI.

He rose and paced the room. "What a hypocrite." He spoke to the image of her in his head. "You ranted at me for selling you out." His jaw tightened. "You lied about being a party girl. Wait. Aaron had lied." His hands fisted. "Maybe I should threaten to punch him in the face."

Marc stalked out of his office, running his fingers through his hair as he headed to the kitchen. "I'm an idiot. Falling in love with a Janet-clone."

The house was dark, and he stumbled on a Lego in the hallway. The pain in his foot matched the pain in his heart. He flicked on the light in the kitchen. The clock on the stove flashed two a.m. Since tucking Tyler into bed, he'd spent hours scouring the internet to discover Bria of the past.

Brownie padded into the kitchen and nudged his hand with his head. Marc patted the dog and then leaned down to pet him. Soon he was sitting on the floor and leaning against the counter with Brownie in his lap. Stroking the dog calmed him. Bria had broken up with him. No, stepped back.

Did he want her in Tyler's life? In the months he'd known her she'd been nothing but kind. She'd never drank. Maybe it was all pretending. *Don't models take on personas?* Why would Aaron bother to seek him out and encourage him to pursue her?

Marc's mind whirled with confusion. *Father, what do I do now? Confront her? Trust her that the past is the past?* Brownie nuzzled close, his presence drawing the anxiety from him. Marc dug his fingers deep into his fur. "Should I punch Aaron in the face?" Marc chuckled as more tension released. Brownie licked his face. "Want to go out?" Brownie stared up at him. At this moment, Marc understood the connection between Tyler and this dog. He stroked his back.

"Thanks for being there for Tyler." He rubbed the space between the dog's eyes. "Thanks for being here for me."

They rose from the floor, and Marc opened the back door. The two stood in the moonlight. Marc stared at the stars. A cold breeze surrounded him. He took a deep breath of the chilled night air allowing it to dislodge the angst he let circle his mind. Brownie explored the yard, then came to stand beside him. The chill in the spring night ruffled his hair and shivered through his body.

"Fear." He patted Brownie's head.

"I'm afraid of making the same mistake."

The dog woofed.

"Let's go inside."

Brownie walked with him into the house. His mind tossed around every memory of Bria, weighing her reaction against Janet's behaviors. He brushed his teeth and scowled at himself in the mirror. The whole time, Brownie stayed by his side. "Don't be a fool." His reflection shared his hurt. He changed for bed and crawled under the covers. Brownie jumped up beside him.

"Seriously, dude. I need some space." Brownie's gaze begged. "Stop it."

Brownie laid his head on his paws. "Not sleeping in my bed." Marc pointed toward the door. "Get off. Go!"

Brownie jumped off and curled on the floor beside the bed.

Marc lay there in the darkness. God had bought both Brownie and Bria into his life at just the right time. Brownie was exactly what Tyler needed. Was Bria? Marc turned to his side and waited for sleep to claim him.

15

Bria threw the red frisbee with the BowWow Rescue logo high in the air. Lizzy, an American Staffordshire, leaped after it grabbing it in her mouth and racing it back to Bria. "Good girl." Bria rubbed the brindle-colored dog. Lizzy had been here longer than most and with the shortage of foster homes, she'd become the center's mascot. The kindly dog had been dropped off when its owner moved to a no-pit bull community.

"You're a sweet girl, yes you are." Bria put her back in her cage and took out Nicco, a malamute/huskie mix and spent a half-hour playing frisbee with him. An afternoon with her furry besties drew her mind away from the mess that piled up concerning a certain man and his adorable son.

"Hey, Bria." Clara stuck her head out the backdoor of the center. "Got a minute?"

"Sure, let me put Nicco away." She did not want to talk about BowWow Rescue's finances. Not today. But she'd ignored Clara's calls and texts over the past week because her head was not in the game. She scrubbed Nicco between the eyes a few times causing his tongue to hang out in enjoyment. "Sorry, but you've got to get back in your cage."

The large dog whined when she put on his leash and then he insisted on walking like an arthritic old man. She'd not brought any treats, a sure-fire way of getting dogs to cooperate. Instead, she matched his pace until at last he was in his cage. He plopped on the floor with a grunt and placed his head on his paws.

"I know exactly how you feel." She sighed and strolled toward the office.

"What's up, Clara?" Bria smiled at the middle-aged woman. Then she spent the next hour going over the budget and the money needed from the upcoming fundraiser to finance the center for the next year. The numbers made her head spin.

"Do you have any ideas for the fundraiser? We need to get flyers out soon." Clara pulled out her notebook.

"I know. I have no clue. Maybe some of the other board members do. I'll call a meeting. No worries." Bria's shoulder's ached with the heavy weight of planning a successful fundraiser. Her creative juices were null. Perhaps by the next board meeting someone would have a great idea that would raise a ton of money. Perhaps spending a bit of time away from dogs and the center would bring on the ideas.

Tomorrow she was spending time with Tyler. It would be the first time they did anything together without Marc. She hoped Tyler enjoyed what she'd planned for their day together.

She frowned at the prospect of taking on the responsibility alone. It had been years since she'd babysat. Until she figured out what her relationship with Marc was—and if she could trust him—there was no other way.

~

"SHE'S COMING, DADDY." Tyler's firm grip on the living room curtain loosened, causing the blinds beneath to rock. "I'm excited." He danced around and clapped his hands.

"I would never have guessed." Marc laughed and grabbed his son's arm as he passed him on the way to the door. "Calm down, sport." Tyler's attachment to Bria made holding her at arm's length challenging. But it was what it was, and Bria's presence in his son's life was important.

Tyler nodded and took a deep breath. The doorbell rang, and Tyler scurried to open it. "Miss Bria." He gave her a bright smile and took her hand.. "Let's go."

Bria wore a pink t-shirt with a Wonder Woman logo paired with jeans and pink sneakers. Her curly thick hair hung around her shoulders. Her skin looked sun-kissed even without make-up.

Marc's heart stilled.

Bria returned Tyler's hug and gave Marc a nervous smile. "In a minute, we'll go." She pulled Tyler's arms loose and turned her lovely eyes on him. Aw, but she was breathtaking. He resisted the urge to hug her too.

"Thanks for doing this." He'd texted and asked if she could entertain Tyler for a few hours today. She'd taken the day off to spend with him. Saturdays were their busiest day. She must really love his son. A jealous ache filled his chest.

"I'm taking Tyler to the mall. There is an activity area there, as well as the Painted Pony." She looked down at his son, her loose-hanging hair covering her face as she focused on Tyler. "After seeing your fine work at creating Brownie from clay, I thought you might like to paint ceramics."

"What's that?" Tyler took her hand and stared up at her.

"Let's see...."

Marc tried not to stare at her thoughtful expression too long. Is this what their friendship would be like? She'd pick up Tyler, and he'd be on the sidelines?

"The best way to explain ceramic is dry clay ready to paint."

Bria's bracelet tinkled as she pushed hair from her face and smiled Marc's way. "Lots of figurines...shapes to choose from. They give us the paint and instructions."

"Cool." Tyler pointed at her T-shirt. "We're both superheroes."

Tyler's shirt had Spiderman on the front.

"I thought of you when I picked it out this morning." She raised her eyebrow at Marc.

He blushed, remembering their morning encounter when she returned Brownie. He'd avoided wearing the Superman pajamas since then. Bria's eyes sparkled with unushered mirth, making the moment less awkward.

"Thanks again, we really appreciate this. Grammie has a doctor's appointment, and I have a meeting with a client." Marc hadn't told Tyler he'd arranged the playdate. What other woman would take a day off work for a kid when she had no interest in the father? *Let it go.*

"I'm glad it's Saturday, no school." Tyler tugged Bria's hand. "Can we go now?"

Marc stretched out his arms, and Tyler dropped her hand and hugged him. "I'll be extra special good. I promise."

Marc secured Tyler's car seat into Bria's car. "Give the latch a little tug to be sure it's tight. Tyler has pulled his arms out of the harness more times than I can count. Don't let him have too many sweets. And...." He gazed into her smiling eyes, and his thought-train jumped the track. He stepped away and shut the car door. "Don't let him control you. He's good at pouting and throwing fits if it suits him."

She looked so gorgeous in her t-shirt and jeans. She was as beautiful in her simplicity as she had been in her black dress. That memory had soured a bit after the misunderstanding. "If he doesn't behave, bring him right home. He's promised to be good. But...you've seen him get sassy when he's tired."

"Don't worry, father hen. I think we'll be fine." She patted his arm. The warmth of her touch fought the friendship banner under which they now stood.

~

TYLER HELD Bria's hand as they entered the mall. A candy kiosk stood between them and the Painted Pony. "May I please have some cotton candy?" The excitement in his face made her an easy target.

"Sure." She purchased a small bag. "Let's sit here while you eat it. I don't think food is allowed in the Painted Pony."

Tyler took a few bites and then handed her the bag. "I'm full. I guess I had too much lunch."

Bria put it in her tote bag. She took Tyler's hand, and stickiness transferred from his fingers to hers.

"Let's find a restroom so you can wash your hands."

"There's one." Tyler pointed to the men's room.

"I can't go in there with you." Panic rose at the idea of standing outside waiting for him.

"I don't want to go into the girl's bathroom." Tyler wrinkled his nose. Bria almost insisted when she saw the family restroom just next door.

She locked the door behind them as Tyler washed his hands at the sink. Then she did the same. Crisis averted. "What do you want to do first?"

"I want to paint."

They entered the Painted Pony and were directed to shelves of ceramic figurines. "Look at all the dogs." Bria headed toward that shelf.

"Wait. I want that horse." Tyler pointed to a figurine of a horse standing on his back legs with a flowing mane.

"Are you sure?"

"Yes. I have a dog. Now I want a horsey."

Bria shoulder-hugged him. "Okay."

"What are you painting?"

Bria chose a rooster.

"Do you want chickens?"

"It's for my mom. Her birthday is coming. When I was a little girl, I made a rooster in art class and gave it to my mom. She still has it."

"Can I see it?"

"Next time we're out at the farm." *Why'd I say that?* This time with Tyler was the first step toward a *friendship* with a man. A wonderful, attractive, caring man. Could she be just friends? Could Tyler be a part of her life without Marc? She restrained a sigh and took the figurines to the counter. After paying for them, an employee gave them each an apron and set them up at a table with paint. Tyler chattered as he painted the body brown and the mane and legs black. He jumped from topic to topic. "What's your favorite dog?"

Bria added green to the tail feathers on her rooster. "My favorite dog was Clarence, my collie. He was a blue-ribbon champion."

"He must have been really smart."

"Yes, and so handsome." Bria rinsed her brush and started adding red to the tail feathers. "I miss him every day."

"Did he run away and get lost?"

"No, he died."

Tyler touched her arm. "That's sad. I would cry a lot if Brownie died."

They painted in silence for a while. Bria finished her project and helped Tyler touch up the spots he'd missed on his horse. "Now we leave them here to be baked, and then I'll pick them up later."

"Today?"

"I don't think so. It takes hours to bake, and there are other projects ahead of ours. Let's ask the clerk."

The teenage girl at the counter convinced Tyler nothing would happen to his horse while in their care and gave Bria a claim ticket. Tyler took Bria's hand and they left the Painted Pony.

"What would you like to do now?"

"Can we ride the merry-go-round?"

Bria bought the tickets, and they rode it twice. Tyler picked a different mount each time.

"Now what?"

Tyler's head drooped. "Can we go home now?'

"Don't you want ice cream?"

"No. I'm still full." Tyler leaned against her. "I had so much fun doing stuff with you. Thank you for taking me." He hugged her. "I'm tired."

She'd never seen Tyler admit he was tired. "I enjoyed being with you, too. Let's go."

~

MARC WRESTLED with a persistent weed in Grammie's gladiola bed. His meeting had secured him another contract, and now he needed to let his mind relax. Weeding provided the perfect mindless activity. Grammie was pruning her roses when Bria pulled into the driveway.

Marc stood and peeled off his gardening gloves. "Hey, you're back early." He opened the back door as Bria turned off the car. "Come on, sport."

"Daddy, my tummy hurts." Tyler's eyes were glassy. Worry shot through Marc. What had Bria let him eat?

"Give me a minute to get you out." Marc struggled with the seatbelt. Tyler didn't fuss.

Marc helped him out. Before Tyler's feet hit the ground, he vomited blue goo on the yard and Marc's sneakers.

Bria rushed to his side. "Tyler, are you all right?"

"I don't feel good." Tyler leaned against Marc.

Marc glared at Bria. *Unbelievable.* Janet's face replaced Bria's as he steadied his son beside him. "What were you thinking feeding him a bunch of junk? I specifically told you not too." Anger seared through him. "You're not winning my trust with a stunt like this."

"A stunt like this?" Hurt flittered across her face for a nanosecond before she pierced him with a scowl. She pulled out a bag of cotton candy from her tote. "Two bites. That was all he ate. Two bites." She thrust the bag to Marc. "Tyler is special to me. I'd never do anything to make him sick."

"Stop." Tyler began to cry.

Bria reached for Tyler and rubbed his back. "I'm sorry."

Marc picked him up.

"Don't yell." Tyler vomited on his shirt. "Sorry, Daddy."

Grammie took Tyler from Marc and placed her hand on his forehead. "I'm sure Bria didn't give him this fever." Her look told him what an idiot he was. "Come on, baby, Grammie will give you a bath."

How could he take back his stupid remark? Moisture rested in Bria's eyes, making him feel worse. "I'm...."

She held up her hand. Silence reigned.

Bria opened the back door and wrestled with the car seat. Marc reached across her and jerked it free. She crossed her arms and pierced him with the same angry look he'd seen when she accused him of selling her out to the paparazzi.

"If you don't want to be friends, just say so. Don't use Tyler as an excuse to put distance between us." She climbed in her car and drove the two blocks to her house, where the garage door opened and enclosed her from his stupidity.

Father, why? Why do I expect Bria to be like Janet? How do I fix this?

He went into the house and texted an apology to Bria. She never responded.

MARC DROPPED Tyler off at school on Monday, then went to the florist and purchased yellow roses for Bria. The florist said they represented friendship. After a night of wrestling both sides of the tally sheet, he decided Bria was worth fighting for. Her past was just that. She wasn't Brittany anymore. Tyler loved her and needed her in his life.

Marc needed her, too.

If Janet had tried to change.... The idea of friendship felt like the wrong colors applied to a romantic website. Yet it was better than having no Bria in his life.

He took the flowers to the dog grooming shop. Aaron came out from the back. "Are those for me?" Aaron put his hand over his heart. "You shouldn't have."

"I didn't. Is Bria here?"

"She's went to pick up her scissors. There's a guy who sharpens our scissors and blades. He called late yesterday to say they're ready,"

"These are for her." He set the bouquet on the counter.

"I'm crushed." Aaron laughed. "Hey, I could use your help with something."

"Yeah?" Marc's mind raced to the things he needed to get done today.

"In two weeks, I'm going to Chicago to compete in the national dog grooming competition. We could use someone to handle the front desk.

All the grooming will fall on Bria, so I thought if you answered the phones and stuff, she'd avoid insanity."

"You realize I have a business." It was so irritating that everyone assumed he had free time because he worked from home. But a week with Bria could be a game changer. He needed to erase the jerk vision hanging between them. "I know nothing about running a shop."

"I see your armor is cracking. Look, you need time with my sister." Aaron didn't mince words.

"She tell you about...?"

"Yeah. Again, misunderstandings can be worked out."

"I hope you're right."

"She needs you around." Aaron's matchmaking skills might work to Marc's advantage. Bria might cross over to the romantic side. "I'll give you a crash course in our computer software and our client cards and you'll be fine."

"And if I say no?"

"Bria will go insane." Aaron grinned. "I plan on winning it all this year. I've been training for it."

"Why would you do that to Bria?"

"Bria agreed to run the shop alone whenever I compete. The trophies bring in customers."

"How do you train for a grooming competition?

"I groom two dogs for free to practice. A poodle and cocker spaniel will go to Chicago with me where I'll create my masterpieces. My mom finished my costume yesterday."

"Competitive grooming is way more than I ever imagined. What's your costume?"

"I'll be Aquaman and Penny, the poodle, will be a seahorse in the design competition. Frank, the cocker spaniel, will be in the grooming competition." Aaron pulled out his phone and showed Marc the design for Penny. The cut and coloring turned a poodle into a sea horse. "I'm going to rock it," he poked a finger at Marc, "and you're going to hold down the fort."

Marc ran his fingers through his hair at Aaron's knowing grin. If only he had the man's gift of mind-reading, then maybe he wouldn't say stupid things to Bria.

∾

"Mr. Martinez, your website's finished." Marc called the latest client. "I have a full plate next week." Marc drummed a pencil on his desk. "Yes, review it today, and I'll get right on the changes. Your website can go live tomorrow."

Marc sighed as the last project for the month neared completion. Under other circumstances, he'd call clients to schedule for next month and start on them early. Instead, he was taking a chance that time with Bria would prove to her...he wasn't sure what. Changing her mind about the friendship thing was his only goal.

"Daddy, do you work for Miss Bria today?" Tyler met him in the hall as he left his office.

"No, son, I start Monday." Marc ruffled his hair. "Why are you so excited that I'm helping Miss Bria?"

"I really, really like her, and she needs to really, really like you." Tyler gripped a toy car against his chest. "Maybe she will forgive you, and we can do stuff together again."

"Maybe." Marc's chest tightened. Tyler's attachment to Bria both warmed and frightened him. If this week went south, it would devastate Tyler. As friends, she'd left the door open for Tyler. If she stepped into the get-out-of-his-life zone...he pulled his mind away from the negative. "Grammie will have to pick you up from school this week. Is that okay?"

"As long as you're home for dinner so you can help with my homework, it's okay." Tyler puckered his lips and his eyebrows dropped, a sure sign he was deep in thought. "I'll make her chocolate chip cookies and maybe brownies too."

"I'm sure she'll love them."

Brownie woofed. Tyler and he raced outside to play.

Marc entered the living room and flopped in his recliner. He reached for the small three-ring binder he'd created to keep track of all the stuff Aaron showed him last night. When she'd returned with the scissors, Bria's reaction to his daily presence while Aaron was away had been unreadable. *Father, I hope this isn't a mistake.*

16

Bria touched up her lip gloss after drinking her chai latte. She studied her reflection in the mirror. Her brush sat on the edge of the tiny sink in the break-room bathroom. She'd brushed out her ponytail, then changed it to a messy bun, then back to a ponytail. Her final decision landed on a quick braid, starting at the crown of her head and descending to her shoulders.

The doorbell tinkled and Marc stood in the doorway, looking fine in jeans and a pink Doggie Designer Duo t-shirt. Her mouth went dry. *Pull it together.* The roses, and the few funny emoji text messages that followed, had gone a long way to healing her wounded feelings. The distance made it easier to forgive him. They hadn't spoken since Tyler'd thrown up. "Hey, Marc."

"Hey, Bria." His smile sent a delicious shiver through her. "I'm ready to work."

She shook her head to refocus from her desire to run into his arms to the business at hand. "Did Aaron explain our opening routine?"

"Yep, right down to the impromptu dance moves." Marc chuckled, then held out his notebook. "Got my cheat sheets here."

"The first appointment's not for an hour." Bria turned on the computer and pulled up their website. "Lloyd will be here soon. He lives upstairs. I told you that, right?" *Stop blabbering.* She found her more professional tone and continued.

"Lloyd and I will get the back room ready while you check the voicemail and the website for added appointments. Call them and confirm or rearrange appointments."

"Why rearrange?" Marc opened his notebook and took out a pen.

"Clients can make online appointments that are unrealistic." Bria pulled up the appointment screen. "Appointments in green are online additions. You'll need to compare them to our client cards." She clicked near a name and a block of information appeared. Marc leaned closer, his woodsy scent inviting.

Moving over a bit she pointed at the information. "See the notes? This appointment is for a bath and an FFF. That's code for face, feet, and fanny. Chico is a beagle, so that appointment is fine. Lloyd does those, so we're good. Chico is booked at the same time as Twilight." She moved the mouse over the notes icon. Twilight's information appeared. "He's a Newfoundland with matted hair."

"I see you added 'crabby' to your notes." Marc leaned in closer. Bria backed away to regain her composure.

"Yes, we remind ourselves of their disposition. A Newfoundland has long hair, and it takes time to groom one. And Twilight complains the whole time."

Bria took in a cleansing breath and patted Marc's arm.

"Thanks for rearranging your schedule to help me. Aaron needs to do these competitions. It's good for business, and it's good for him too. He is an awesome artist, and the contest is a great outlet for him. I kinda lost it two years ago when I manned the shop alone. I couldn't ask him to skip this year too."

He squeezed her shoulder. "Always happy to help a friend." His emphasis on the word friend wasn't gelling with her heart reaction when his touch sent a tingle from her shoulder to her toes..

The doorbell rang, giving her a chance to step away from Marc. "Jerry, what happened to Star?" The dog's snow-white coat stuck out in various directions on her left side. The dog's appearance resembled Bria's emotions with her new receptionist.

She turned to Marc. "Star is a Great Pyrenees. You'd never know it now." She ran her hands over the irregular coat. Star's gaze beamed sadly as she leaned in for a snuggle. "Poor baby."

"I've apologized to Star a few times and to my wife and daughters." Jerry's sheepish look confirmed his remorse. "The wife and I were looking for ways to trim the budget. I got this brilliant idea to groom Star myself."

He patted her head. "I watched a YouTube video. The guy made it look so easy." Jerry sighed. "The dog he groomed stood still as a statue. He never mentioned dogs move so much."

"Star is a wiggler." Bria chuckled. "Poor thing. I'll have to shave her down."

"Can you do it today?" Jerry looked at his watch. "I need to get to work."

"Marc, what's the schedule like?" Bria had checked the schedule from home but wanted to test Marc's copious notes.

"At ten you could fit her in." Marc looked at her for confirmation.

Bria took the leash from Jerry. "You can come get her after work."

"Thanks. I'll cut my golfing to twice a month, so Star gets the best." Jerry waved as he left. Buoyed by Jerry's compliment, her nervousness dissolved.

Bria's first client, a Boston terrier, entered. He dragged Amanda, his owner, into the front lobby and headed toward Star.

"Give me a minute." She held up one finger to Amanda and took Star to a crate before the two dogs could begin their smelling ritual.

She returned and squatted before the little black dog with a pug nose. He licked her face and snorted, then piddled. Bria fished a treat from her jean pocket.

"Hey, Terrance." Bria gave him the treat. "Ready for your bath?" Terrance let out a wail that made Marc and Amanda laugh. A pool formed around his paws.

"Marc, thanks again for helping." She grinned while he reached under the counter for paper towels and cleaner.

"All part of the job." Marc pasted on a smile she knew was for the client.

Having someone else to clean up accidents was a nice perk.

Keeping busy helped her forget Marc was there. Almost. She put in her earbuds and cranked up the worship music on her iPhone. It took her mind off the handsome man who'd come to her aid. Worrying about having the whole responsibility for the shop had robbed her of sleep, until Aaron had arranged for Marc to man the front desk. *Maybe if today goes smoothly, I can finally get a good night's sleep.* Unless she dreamed of a blond man willing to wear a pink t-shirt.

～

MARC READ each info card details before confirming or changing an appointment. He wanted to impress Bria with his efficiency. "This isn't too hard."

He finished the task between phone calls. The phone rang incessantly. Marc did his best to sound friendly and professional as he booked appointments. Aaron had said to leave space for emergencies. Star wasn't the kind of emergency Marc had imagined.

Four other dogs arrived. Marc cleaned urine off the floor after a frightened German shepherd played tug-of-war with Lloyd. The bather won and coaxed the dog into the tub. Yep, Aaron had left no stone unturned in sharing all the potential scenarios of maintaining the front lobby. He'd mop the floor with bleach-water later.

Bria never left the back room all morning. *So much for spending time together.* He texted Grammie at ten with a plan.

By noon, things had slowed. He stuck his head in the doorway to the grooming room. "The next appointment is at two. Do you want lunch?"

Bria looked up from clipping Ginger the golden retriever's nails. She took her earbuds out when Marc approached her grooming station. "What?" A loose hair drooped in her eyes. Marc moved it behind her ear, causing a blush on Bria's cheeks.

"Want to break for lunch?"

Bria laid her tools aside and tied a lavender floral bandana around Ginger's neck. "Do we have time?"

Marc retrieved Ginger's leash and put it on the dog. "You didn't hear me say your next appointment is at two." He put Ginger in the crate with the card with her name on it.

The doorbell sounded.

"Probably a walk-in." Bria swept the hair from her grooming area.

Marc glanced toward the front door. Right on time. "No, it's Grammie." Marc stepped toward the bathing room where Sherman the Bassett hound was drying in a nearby crate. "Lloyd, you ready for lunch?"

"Don't have to ask me twice." Lloyd dropped a stack of folded towels near the bathing tub. "Hello, Delores." Lloyd took the basket from her hand. "Allow me." He winked at her. "What smells so good?"

Was Grammie blushing? She gave Lloyd a sweet smile. "Chicken salad sandwiches, fresh veggies, and brownies."

"Thank you, ma'am." Lloyd peeked in the basket. "It's a treat to get food prepared by an attractive woman for a change." He grinned, and Marc groaned.

"Come on, Bria, let's eat while we can." Marc jerked the basket from Lloyd's hand and set it on the break table.

"Are you staying?" Lloyd asked Grammie.

"No, I've a few errands before I pick up Tyler. Enjoy your lunch. Marc, please bring the basket home so I can use it tomorrow." Grammie's cheeks were still pink on her way out.

"Is she planning on bringing lunch every day?" Bria grabbed paper plates from her stash. Cinco de Mayo blazed across the red and yellow surface. "She doesn't need to."

"Aaron made me promise you'd eat every day. Grammie's happy to bring food. She worried I wouldn't have time to eat, so she volunteered. A win-win." Marc bit into his sandwich. It was a little white lie—but Grammie happily supported Marc's endeavor to win Bria away from the dark side. "Her chicken salad is awesome. It won a recipe contest."

"She enters her recipes in contests?" Bria took a bite. The delight on her face and quiet sigh pleased Marc. "When did she win?"

"I think it was when my mom was a kid. She has the newspaper article framed. The prize was a hundred dollars, and her recipe is in a sandwich cookbook."

"Your grandmother is something." Lloyd shoved the last bite of sandwich in his mouth. "Hey, don't look at me like that."

Marc realized he was wearing the don't-even-think-about-it stare he gave Tyler when he took his crayons to draw on the wall. "Sorry"

"I get it. But she's a gracious lady who deserves compliments mixed with a little flirting." Lloyd grinned, but Marc didn't care for the explanation.

Bria came to the rescue. "This is the twenty-first century, women don't want shallow compliments mixed with flirting. It's not fair to give a false impression."

"Well, Delores and I are old enough to understand a bit of fun." Lloyd dipped a carrot in dressing. "I'll be more businesslike the next time. You should speak to your brother. He flirts with the female clients."

"Only Mrs. Rogers." Bria pointed a broccoli spear at him. "She's eighty-five and flirts with every man she sees." She popped the vegetable in her mouth.

"True, she loves it." Lloyd laughed, then turned to Marc. "How are you liking your first day?"

"Other than mopping up nervousness, it's not been too bad." Marc smiled at Bria and choked on a carrot when she winked at him. Was she flirting or just teasing about his fun job?

"You okay?" Bria patted his back and handed him a bottle of water.

"I'm fine." Marc's cheeks warmed from more than the errant vegetable. He sipped the water in sheepish silence. *Hold it together man.* Aaron's plan might just be working.

"Time to get back to business." Bria grabbed the trash and empty paper plates.

"Wait." Marc opened the Tupperware container of brownies. She groaned as she reached, then retracted her hand a few times before giving in.

Bria grabbed the frosted treat as if they might be taken away at any moment. She sat back in her chair with a napkin secured in her lap to enjoy the decadent dessert. "This single brownie will add twenty pounds."

"You work way too hard for those imaginary pounds to cling to you." He admired her perfect form for a moment. "Consider it a perk for having me here. Grammie's bringing dessert every day."

"You should tell her not to," Bria protested as she snatched a second brownie.

"Can I have what's left?" Lloyd bit into his fourth.

"Can you leave one for me?" Marc laughed. "I'm not telling my grand-mother that her desserts are unwelcome because Bria Willis gains twenty pounds with every bite."

"Okay, fine." Bria wiped frosting from her lips. "I'll need to exercise more restraint." Her piercing look seemed to refer to more than dessert. Maybe he was ripping a few bricks from the wall around her heart. He'd asked Grammie to make her outstanding lemon squares. Was the way to this woman's heart through her sweet tooth?

17

Marc found Bria's continuing coolness toward him puzzling. Efficiently running the front desk, cleaning up dog anxiety in the lobby, and plying her with sweets hadn't won him the accolades he'd hoped. It was Friday, Saturday was the end of the week-long commitment, and the frost in the air was disparaging.

The doorbell rang. A man dressed in Ralph Lauren slacks and a polo shirt, with his haircut pristine, stepped up to the counter. Why did he look familiar? Where was his dog?

"Is Bria Willis in?"

Marc connected the man to the tabloid photo. He tried to maintain a neutral face. "Mr. Treat?"

"Call me Mitch." He held out his hand.

"You need to leave." Marc puffed out his chest, attempting to look as intimidating as possible while wearing a pink t-shirt. "Bria doesn't want to see you."

"Who are you—her boyfriend or something?" Mitch's smirk irked Marc.

"Or something." Marc hoped the answer didn't sound weak.

Bria came from the back room, tendrils of hair framing her face. Dog fur dusted her smock. "Is there a problem?" Rufus, a black Doberman, stood beside her. His low growl caused Mitch to step back and hold up his hands.

"Listen, I don't want any trouble."

Fisting her hands, she glared. "Mitch, turn around and walk back out of my life."

"Man, you've really let yourself go." Mitch scanned her form. "Put on makeup and a sexy dress, fix your hair. I've got an offer you'd be a fool to refuse."

Bria stepped close and crossed her arms. "Let me spell it out for you. N.O."

Mitch grabbed her arm. "Don't be a ..."

"A fool." Bria glared and tried to pull away.

Marc rammed himself between the two, forcing Mitch to release her. "You heard her." Grabbing the front of Mitch's expensive shirt, Marc twisted the fabric to maintain a tight grip.

"Get out of my face. I'll have you arrested." Mitch's growl sounded weak compared to Rufus' response. The dog remained close by, a low growl of warning as he glared at the man. Marc shoved Mitch back and moved to Bria's side. Mitch stepped back, giving Bria a fiery stare. "You owe me."

"What?" Anger flashed in her eyes.

Marc placed his hand on the small of her back. Mitchell glared at her.

"You know, I lost a lot of money when you bailed. Finding replacements to fill those contracts cost a bundle. Then the movie deal went down the toilet. My name lost creds. You wrecked my career."

Marc could feel the intimidation Mitch focused her way. Bria seemed to struggle to find her voice as unushered tears glistened. "I lost something very precious that day I ended up in the ER."

Marc's chest tightened with her grief. He wrapped his arm around her waist. Bria leaned into him for a moment, her shiver raced right to his heart. He would do anything to protect her. But she straightened, left the safety of his arms and took a step toward her ex.

"When I left the hospital, I went straight to my parent's house and never looked back. You're lucky the police weren't involved after you pushed me. If you try one more time to manipulate me to go back, I'll press charges against you."

Mitch's face paled. He looked toward the front window in silence. When he turned back to her his eyes pleaded. "Can you show a guy a little mercy here? If you would come back for one job... I need this gig. I'm on the verge of bankruptcy."

Bria chewed her lower lip for a nanosecond before touching Marc's arm. "Call the police."

Marc gripped the phone. "You've got ten seconds to leave before I make this call."

Mitch's eyes widened. "You're really not going to help?"

"You can't convince me for one minute that my leaving five years ago brought you to bankruptcy. Knowing you, you've overextended your credit and are living above your means. That is your problem—not mine. There is no scenario where I would return to that life." Bria pointed to the exit.

Mitchell's shoulders sagged and something resembling regret rested in his eyes. At the door, the man turned toward her. "For what it's worth. I'm sorry. If I had a do-over, things would be different. Bye, Bria."

Marc stepped to the window and watched him head to his car. She joined him there and took his hand. "Thanks for being here. You stood up for me. That means a lot."

Before Marc could pull her close, she stepped away and turned to Rufus. "You know Rufus is a 'fraidy cat?"

Marc chuckled. "His growl didn't give that impression" His laughter removed the anxiety from the room and brought a smile to Bria's face.

He gazed at her. "I'd do anything to keep you safe. I promised Aaron I'd watch out for you while he was gone."

"Two bodyguards are more than enough." Bria stroked Rufus and rewarded him with a treat. "You're my hero."

"What am I, cheesecake?" Marc laughed.

"Absolutely, sweet and smothered in goodness." She kissed Rufus' head and came to Marc, brushing his cheek with her lips and lingering in a comfortable embrace for a moment. The smell of dog shampoo reminded Marc they were at work and to rein in his desire to kiss her. Bria pulled back, and her gaze rested on him. "You are so above me in so many ways." Was that shame in her eyes?

Marc resisted the temptation to argue the point. "Lloyd should be here any minute with the Subway sandwiches." Bria needed a distraction and time to process this alone. "Today Grammie's at her Bible study group."

Bria took a deep breath and offered a sweet smile. "Sounds great. I've finished Rufus. Call his dad."

The doorbell rang again, and Lloyd handed over the sandwiches. While they ate, Lloyd entertained them with stories from his childhood of growing up with four brothers in an apartment in Queens, New York. Marc laughed in all the right places, but his heart grieved for Bria. *What did she lose in the hospital?*

"Hey." Bria pulled her phone from her pocket. "Look." She showed the guys her phone. Aaron, a.k.a. Aquaman, and his now-transformed seahorse, posed with a large trophy.

"He won best of show in artistic design. He wrote, 'The lady judges were giving me the eye when I flexed my muscles. LOL! Frank and me won first in cocker spaniel cuts, but a poodle won best of show. All male judges.'" He'd added a smiley face emoji with muscular arms.

Bria pocketed her phone. "He'll be home sometime today, but I doubt he'll show up at the shop."

"Why not? Won't he want to show off his trophy?" Lloyd asked.

"The body paint leaves a colorful stain for a few days. He'll bring the trophy in Monday."

"I'd like to see Aaron slightly green." Lloyd chuckled, clearing more tension from the air.

18

Thursday morning, Bria arrived early at work. She'd swung by the coffee shop and bought scones and coffee. Marc had been so thoughtful to provide lunch. Or rather, Delores had. Bria wanted to return the kindness. The guy sure knew how to run the front office. Marc kept the shop's pot of coffee fresh and even brought in a new case of water for the fridge. Then he bought more beach towels for their larger clients. How the man had managed to grab her phone and download a new song mix was a mystery. Definitely not part of his job description, but oh so sweet.

When she set the coffee and scones on the counter, she found the wilted roses had been replaced with daisies. Marc had more than pitched in where needed. The man was amazing.

Lloyd and Marc entered. She held out her offering.

"Thanks, boss." Lloyd grabbed a cup.

"Goes great with these." Marc opened a box of donuts. "Great minds think alike. And don't mention fattening, you look fantastic."

"I already ate breakfast," Bria countered, carrying the cardboard coffee carrier to the trash.

"More for the men." Marc grabbed a scone and sat at the tall stool behind the counter.

"Wait." Bria took a chocolate-glazed donut and pointed at Marc. "Bad influence."

Marc wiggled his eyebrows and smiled.

"I'm telling Delores." Bria bit into the confection.

"She provided the coupon."

Bria feigned a shocked expression and marched to the back room before a second donut called. The man was becoming as addictive as the sweet treats. Marc made her feel...cherished. The idea of opening up to more than friendship again flittered through her head.

Marc brought Brutus, a pit bull mix to the back. He skittered along the floor as Brownie had done the first day. Marc signal heel, and Brutus obeyed.

"Good boy." Marc patted the canine's head gingerly. "Wasn't sure Brutus knew the same signals as Brownie." He handed the leash over to Lloyd, who took the dog back to the bathing room. "His mom's coming back at three."

"Plenty of time." Bria smiled. "My, my, you've adopted groomers' lingo, calling the client's owner, 'mom.'"

"Bad influence." Marc grinned and ran his finger down her arm, producing a delightful shiver.

The doorbell rang and Madonna the Maltese with her sister, Whitney the schnauzer, arrived. Their owner, Blair, sidestepped to avoid getting tangled in the leashes.

"I apologize in advance for not walking them. I'm almost running late for work." Blair handed their leashes to Marc and headed out the door. The dogs piddled at his feet.

"I guess I'm the potty whisperer." Marc scowled. "Is it normal to clean up this much pee?"

"We have weeks like this. The full moon brings more poo deposits." Bria laughed at his eye-roll. "You bring out the best in our clients." Bria winked, and Marc moaned. "Walk those two and put them in a crate together. They'll be calmer that way."

Marc took the pair out while Bria grabbed the paper towels and cleaned the floor. The bell tinkled, and a wet tongue greeted Bria's face. "Brownie, what are you doing here?"

"Tyler insisted on bringing his homemade cookies right away." Delores pulled on Brownie's leash to no avail. Tyler gave the heel signal, and he settled.

"I told you, Grammie, don't jerk on the leash." Tyler gave an exasperated sigh, then smiled at Bria and offered his treat. "They're the best warm."

"Thank you, sweetheart." Bria put the cookies on the counter and gave him a hug. "I've missed you."

"Really?" Tyler hugged tighter. "I thought you were still mad at me."

"I was never mad at you." Bria held the boy at arm's length and stared into his innocent eyes. "Why would you think that?"

"'Cause after I threw up on Daddy, I never saw you again." Tyler's eyes glistened.

"Honey, I'm sorry. I've been busy with the shop and working at the animal shelter. I thought you knew...." *How foolish to assume a child would know.* "Tyler, I love you. You're a great friend."

"I'm glad. I thought I made you mad like Mommy."

"What are you talking about, sport?" Marc came from the backroom and pulled him to his side.

"When I was in the car with Mommy, she was mad at me. I never got to say sorry for making her mad." Moisture streamed down Tyler's face.

Marc hugged him. "She knew you were sorry." He stroked Tyler's hair.

Bria's heart melted. *My thoughtlessness caused this boy's pain.*

Delores knelt, before her grandson. "It's not your fault."

Tyler nodded and sniffed.

Bria took his hand. "Forgive me?"

"Yes. You're my bestest grown-up friend in the whole wide world."

"Let's grab a pizza and a movie on Friday." Bria squeezed his hand.

"Cool! Can Daddy come too?" Tyler looked between them.

"Sure. It's a date." Bria knew without looking that the man wore a smug smile. She didn't care. Reconnecting with Tyler was important. After all, she was his bestest grown-up friend. Pain from the past shot through her.

"Don't forget to eat them warm." Tyler pulled her to the counter.

Bria took out a chocolate chip cookie and made appropriate sounds of appreciation. "Wonderful. You're a great baker."

They left after Tyler hugged his dad, and Lloyd gave Brownie a tummy rub.

"Back to work, guys. To borrow Aaron's favorite line, 'I don't want to be here until midnight.' "Bria motioned for Llyod to follow.

Music, normally calming, did nothing as she trimmed Madonna. Tyler's visit had ripped open an old wound. Her baby would have been five this month. Bria sighed and knuckled moisture off her cheek. Her total lack of concern for Tyler's feelings proved she'd never be a good mother. She was barely a good friend to the boy who'd stolen her heart. Tyler deserved so much more. He'd had a mom who focused on her own needs.

Tyler should take first priority for a mom. Did Marc think she'd be a good mother to his son? *Lord, did You bring Tyler to me to help heal my pain? Is Marc Your will for me?* Taking a cleansing breath, she focused back on her client. Her furry friends always brought her comfort when her mind was muddled. Even they couldn't bring her emotions in check. She really need to hear God and not her own fears.

19

F riday morning had flown by with incessant phone calls while Marc
was trying to return other calls.

After lunch, the next client—that Marc could only describe as
a bear—entered. The dog left a large pile of anxiety at the front door and a
trail of wetness as Bria tugged his leash and encouraged him forward with
dog treats.

"Come on, Dexter." Bria's patience amazed Marc. "That's a good boy."
The dog moved a few feet with every treat until they reached the back
room.

The owner's cheeks reddened, but he said nothing as he left. Marc
pulled on latex gloves and grabbed the roll of paper towels, then closed the
half-door between the two rooms to block the dog's retreat. Bria coaxed the
dog to the bathing area.

"What kind of dog is he?"

"I think a Saint Bernard, chow, poodle mix. Only DNA testing would
confirm it." Bria handed the treats to Lloyd. Dexter followed the bather.

Marc finished cleaning the floor when the phone rang. "Hey, sport.
Hang on."

Marc went to Bria. "Tyler is double checking, are we still on for dinner
and a movie tonight?"

Bria changed the blade on her electric shaver and cut a few rows down
a mini-poodle's back before answering. "Sure."

"If you need...."

"Stop." Bria turned off the razor. "Tyler shouldn't be disappointed because my day tottered on the edge of the toilet." She sighed and smiled. "Time with Tyler sounds like the perfect distraction."

"If you're sure?" Marc didn't want the obligation to turn into a disaster for either Bria or his son.

"Tell him I'm looking forward to it." She went back to grooming her client

Marc returned to the phone.

"It's on." Marc smiled at his son's excited, "yes."

The rest of the day remained accident-free—at least in the lobby. During some down-time, Marc reviewed Doggie Designer Duo's less-than-stellar website.

"Hey, Bria." Marc walked back into the grooming room. Bria danced with her earphone cords swaying to a silent beat. He enjoyed her hip movement—a bit too much. She blushed and removed the buds. Marc laughed.

"Need something?" Bria held back a giggle.

He leaned against the doorframe. "Can I upgrade your website?"

"So, you think it's lame too?" Bria chuckled and pushed hair out of her face with her elbow while she held onto Dexter's paw.

"Yep." Marc stepped toward her and held Dexter in place while she switched paws. He kept smiling to mask his fear of the monster-sized canine's teeth.

"Sounds great, but we should ask Aaron. Send him a price quote."

She started to put her earbuds back in, then paused. "Hey, would you be willing to upgrade the website for the Bowwow Rescue? We use the site to help find dogs a forever home. It's really old and hard to change out pictures."

"Send me the link and I'll check it out. Who do I contact?"

"Me. I'm president this year."

"Since when?" Marc knew how passionate she was about their mission, but when did she find the time to be president?

"Since last month's election. Our present president decided not to come back after her baby is born. So as acting president, it became permanent." Bria patted Dexter and tied a Batman bandana around his neck. "We need a better website to promote our annual fundraiser."

"Marketing is what I do."

"Do you?" Bria teased. "We can discuss it after Tyler is in bed."

"It's a plan." Marc smiled and left with a lighter heart at the prospect of more time with Bria. Another chance to be a help to her and maybe show her that they could be good together.

~

MARC HAD REQUESTED a booth in the back corner of Pizza Village, the perfect spot to share a meal and keep Tyler from noticing the antique pinball machines in the side room. Bria had pulled her hair, still damp from a shower, back with a hair band, and she wore just a touch of makeup. The smell of strawberry shampoo and something citrus tickled Marc's nose as Bria fixed her eyes on Tyler. The boy's admiration matched his own.

"Miss Bria, I don't like onions or 'matoes on pizza, and mushrooms are disgusting." Tyler stuck out his tongue and held his stomach. "Yuck!"

"But they're so healthy for a growing boy. Don't you want to grow up big and strong like your daddy?" Bria's smile brought gold flicks to her emerald irises.

"No." Tyler crossed his arms and made a playful grunt.

"Let's order a personal pizza for you. Bria and I will share the other." Marc took the menu away from Tyler as the waitress brought soft drinks.

"Pepperoni and cheese only on mine." Tyler chopped the air with his hand.

"Fine." Marc nodded to the waitress, who added the order to the hand-held computer on her wrist. Then he smiled at Bria. "And what would you like?"

"A supreme with everything." Bria took the paper off her straw. "Don't look so shocked." She laughed. Marc reached over and took her hand briefly, then withdrew it. Her smile never faltered. "They've got the best supreme pizza. Their taco pizza runs a close second."

"How about half supreme and half taco. Make it...."

"Large."

The waitress left and Bria added, "I love cold pizza for breakfast."

"A woman after my heart." Marc winked.

Tyler piped up. "Mine too. I love pizza anytime."

"I don't like just any pizza for breakfast." Bria leaned forward as if sharing a secret. "I never take Mouse Maze pizza home."

"Why?" Tyler's expression of surprise was priceless.

Marc pulled him close and whispered. "Because it's too greasy."

"No." Bria tapped the table, causing the waitress to turn. Bria waved her away and giggled. The sweet tremor of her laugh enveloped their small table in peace.

"Then tell us, Miss Bria." Marc straightened and nodded to Tyler, who joined him in staring at her.

"There are no veggies on Mouse Maze pizzas. Here the cold pizza is like eating a veggie omelet."

Tyler shot her his grossed-out expression. More laughter added another layer of happiness to their gathering. Marc wished he could bottle this moment.

The waitress brought their pizza pies, and after grace, they dug in. Tyler took a bite and then plied Bria with questions, which, before she could answer, he interrupted with his own observations. He jumped from topic to topic between bites. Bria seemed totally invested in every detail of his son's flighty conversation. Maybe she was too tired to put up a fight against his barrage of words. "Miss Bria, I forgot to tell you. I went to the animal shelter with Grammie and my friend Tim and his mom. Tim adopted a cat."

"What did you think of it?"

"So sad. I wanted to take all the dogs and cats home, but Grammie said no." Tyler stuck his lower lip out and then went back to eating.

"Animal shelters do the best they can. Have you ever heard of Bowwow Rescue?" She focused on Marc while directing the question to Tyler. Marc finished his sip of root beer, hoping she wouldn't suggest a visit. Helping at the grooming shop was enough exposure to dogs to last a lifetime.

"What is Bowwow Rescue?" Tyler belched after taking a long sip of soda. He chortled and then quieted at Marc's scowl.

Bria's eyes twinkled while pretending to not notice the burp. "The organization fosters dogs rather than using the animal shelter."

"Walter from my class is a foster kid. He lives with the Martins instead of his real mommy." Tyler's knowledge surprised Marc.

"Did Walter tell you that?"

"Yeah, he was crying at recess, and I ask him why. He said his mommy couldn't take him home yet. But I don't know why." Tyler fell silent. Marc gave him a shoulder hug.

Bria patted his hand.

"The dogs in the rescue program need new homes. Their owners couldn't keep them."

"Like Mr. Lloyd couldn't keep Brownie?"

"That's right. You're pretty smart, you know that?" Bria's praise got a nod from Tyler.

"I know."

"You know?" Marc ruffled his hair. "How about a thank you?"

"Thank you, Miss Bria, for saying I'm smart." The three laughed while the waitress refilled drinks.

"Tyler, look at this." Bria pulled out her phone and flipped to the photo of Aaron in costume.

"Wow! Cool!" Tyler held the phone and stared for several seconds. "He won a really big trophy. Mr. Aaron is very smart too."

"Yes. And that sweet poodle was a rescue. The new owners let Aaron take her to competitions. She loves the attention."

"Can I see her for real?"

"Maybe." Bria put her phone away. She looked at Marc. "Bowwow Rescue's annual fundraiser is coming up fast. Hilary always had it planned a year ahead. She sent out initial save-the-dates six months ago. Right now, she's under doctor's orders to stay in bed for the duration of her pregnancy, and I'm guilty of the too-busy excuse."

"I'd pay to see dogs dressed up." Tyler smiled at the pair. Bria kissed his cheek. "You're an extra-smart boy."

"You plan on having Aaron turn the rescue dogs into seahorses?" Marc asked.

Bria sat deep in thought as she chewed a slice of pizza. She laid it back on her plate and dabbed her lips with a napkin. "No, but almost. The goal of our organization is to find forever homes for these dogs. We take the dogs to various events and let people pet them. Why not give them their own venue?" Bria grabbed a fresh napkin and dug a pen from her purse. "What if we had a fashion show?"

"I'm intrigued." Marc leaned in to see what she wrote.

"We get volunteers to wear matching costumes with the dogs they lead on the runway." Bria pointed at imaginary images. "A poodle led by a woman dressed in a poodle skirt. We could mix the rescues up with other dogs like Officer Jordan and his K-9 partner, Max."

"A Dalmatian in a firemen's helmet?" Marc added.

"Love it. One of our clients is a firefighter. And his wife, Sadie, is on the board and loves to do silent auctions. She has connections to local businesses." Bria jotted a note.

"Hamilton could be a dragon. Like the one from the Training Your Dragon movie," Tyler added.

"Sure. And Aaron's buddy Bob could dress as a Viking. Bob's built like one." Bria grabbed another napkin. "I should have typed this in my phone."

They continued to toss out ideas for costumes as they finished their food.

"Hey, look at the time. We have to hurry to make it to the movie." Marc took out his wallet and handed Bria cash. "Could you pay while I take Tyler to the bathroom?"

"No problem."

Marc hustled Tyler to the bathroom. Two parents made life so much easier. Yep, Bria would be a great mom. He just had to convince her he'd make a good husband.

BRIA HELD the door open as Marc carried Tyler into the house. The boy had fallen asleep during the car ride home from the movie. "Does he wake up once he's in the house?"

"No, he's out until morning." Marc headed toward the stairs. "I'll be right back."

Bria yearned to follow them upstairs and tuck Tyler in bed. But it wasn't her place. And probably never would be.

"How was the movie?" Delores came down the hall in lounge clothes and bunny slippers. "Tea?"

"Yes, please. Marc is putting Tyler to bed. He couldn't stop talking about the movie."

"Until he did." Delores laughed.

"It's so weird, Tyler talks a mile a minute then comes to a screeching halt and falls asleep." Bria shook her head.

"Marc did that as a child." Grannie checked the steeping tea.

Bria never imagined the behavior could be hereditary.

Marc came down the stairs. "Would you believe he woke up? I'll do the bedtime routine and be down in a bit. I hope." He dashed back upstairs.

"Tell me, Bria, how are you and Marc getting along?" Delores' frankness startled her.

Bria adjusted her chair and stared at the tabletop for a moment while the heat left her face.

"I know he's very fond of you."

"I'm very fond of him, but..." Bria whispered as she struggled to express her heart.

"I know you're an answer to my prayers for Marc and Tyler."

"Me?"

"Bria, your mom shared enough about your time as a model for me to understand that look in your eyes." Grammie patted her hand. "We have a very forgiving God. One who erases the past and gives us a new future when we surrender to Him. You've done that. If God has thrown all those years in the sea of forgetfulness, shouldn't you?"

"It's just...Marc is so much above me."

"Really?" Grammie shook her head. "So you get the decide who God has for you based on your worthiness? If that were true, my husband and I would never have married."

Bria wiped a tear with the back of her hand. "It's not the same."

"True, the circumstances were different. Your nightmares are about the child you lost, his were about the lives he took. Your war is different." Delores squeezed her hand. Comfort flowed through her fingers. "God says you're His child and therefore worthy of all the good things He has for you. Don't push that away."

The older woman's words of assurance flowed into Bria's soul. "Thank you. I promise I'll not push away God's leading." Now she needed time to discern if Marc was the direction she was to go. "Don't mention the baby."

"Of course not. I'll be praying." They rose and embraced. Noise on the stairway closed the conversation.

"A miracle, he's out like a light." Marc stood in the kitchen doorway. "What did I miss?"

Bria's heart thumped a betraying rhythm as her cheeks warmed. "Delores was telling me something interesting you did as a child." Bria teased and hoped her eyes weren't red.

"What's that?" Marc joined them in the kitchen.

"Falling asleep in the middle of a sentence." Delores smiled and Marc gave a mock scowl.

"Your memory is fading fast. That was my sister, not me."

"That's right, you were the sleepwalker." Delores placed three mugs on the counter and poured the steeped tea into them.

"Let's just tell all the family secrets." Marc grabbed honey from the cabinet. "Are you going to bring out the naked baby pictures next?"

"Don't tempt me." Grammie gave him a sassy smile.

"Delores, let's have lunch together so you can tell me all his odd habits."

Marc gave a playful groan.

"It's a date." Delores sliced banana bread and placed the plate on the kitchen table. The three took seats. "How did your evening go?" Delores' innocent expression gave away nothing.

"It was fun. We didn't bring left-over pizza home because we didn't want to leave it in the car during the movie." Marc bit into the banana bread.

"Tyler gave me a great idea for the Bowwow Rescue fundraiser." Bria filled her in.

"How clever." Delores snapped her finger. "My book club is looking for a volunteer opportunity. This could be the perfect one. Hattie's been begging us to read...the title escapes me, but it's a story of a dog. How perfect. We had a cupcake bake sale to raise money for the library last year in honor of *The Cupcake Mystery*."

"We can certainly use the volunteers." Bria stared at the sweet woman for a moment. "Are you sure? I mean, it's going to be a lot of work."

"If Grammie heads it up, things will run on time and on point." Marc's praise brought a smile to Delores' face.

"Our book club is more than about reading. It's about community service too." Grammie poured more tea in their half-empty cups.

"If you're sure, I'll text the committee in the morning. They'll be thrilled we have an idea and volunteers lined up. We'll need to move fast. The event is scheduled for July."

"If you're available Sunday afternoon, maybe your board and a few of my fundraising gurus can help get a solid footing under the project." Delores' determination convicted Bria. Like many on the Bowwow Rescue board, she hoped someone else would take charge. Delores had no vested interest in the project, yet here she was stepping up to meet a need. She hoped her friends were as willing.

"I'll ask in my text tomorrow. We can meet at my house." Bria hoped she wasn't the only board member at the last-minute meeting. "I'll call you after work tomorrow and let you know either way."

"I can do an ad campaign on social media and create flyers," Marc offered.

"Are you sure? You've already done so much." Bria tried not to look too eager. Taking advantage of their growing friendship wasn't fair to Marc.

"It's a good cause, and Tyler had the idea." Marc took another slice of banana bread. "It's what dads do."

Just like my dad, volunteering his time for his kids. "Thanks so much." This guy was definitely a keeper. Maybe God had brought him for her. If she could calm her nervous hands long enough to grab hold, maybe she'd get her happily ever after.

~

MARC ARRIVED at the grooming shop to find Bria and Aaron glaring at each other. *Awkward...* Aaron turned to Marc and fixed a smile over a frown. "I see you survived the week."

"Just barely. Nice trophies." Marc stepped behind the counter. The tension between the siblings filled the room. "Are you here for the day?"

"No, I came to tell Bria I hired another groomer, and she throws this dog fashion show at me." Aaron crossed his arms and glared at Marc. "I hear you're all for it."

Marc crossed his own arms prepared to defuse the situation. If a client entered now, they might be tempted to call 911.

"You can't hire anyone without asking me first." Bria stood toe to toe with her bulky brother.

"You can't volunteer me and have the shop closed on a Saturday." Aaron growled. "Not happening."

Bria shoved his shoulder. "I just let you go away for a week and took on the burden of the grooming for something that's important to *you*."

Bria got that same dagger stare from Aaron that Marc had seen from her twice now. *Must be a family trademark.*

Marc didn't dare get between the bickering duo.

Aaron kept his glare locked onto Bria's. Then she changed tactics. Tears glistened in her eyes. She squeezed his shoulder. "Please, it would mean the world to me."

Aaron's resolve started to melt. He inhaled deeply and rubbed the back of his neck. "Ahh, you're right." He shrugged. "I know Bowwow Rescue is a big part of your life. I get it. But these grooming trophies bring in a higher customer volume for weeks after a show."

"Don't you think promoting the rescue will do the same?"

"Maybe." Aaron placed his trophy on the shelf. "Drew is hired. Maybe with his help, we can pull off the Doggie Fashion Show."

Bria sighed. "All right, he can work that Saturday, if I decide he's competent. Even if we have to close the shop, we can reschedule clients, we have time." She brushed stray dog hairs from the front of her shirt. "We can do this. I know we can."

Aaron chuckled. "I guess it's a deal, then."

Bria and Aaron shook hands.

"I'll move his start date to Monday." Aaron headed toward the door. "I'm going home to shower." Aaron pulls up her shirt revealing a tint of his design. "I've already tried showering off the body paint, The green and gold looked awesome, didn't streak but it doesn't rub off easily, used all the makeup remover that came with it. Next time I'm not buying theatrical grade.

Aaron climbed into his SUV as Marc chuckled and shook his head. "Never get me to wear a weird costume." Then he patted Bria's shoulder. "Seems like you guys resolved that pretty well."

"I guess." Bria frowned. "We are supposed to be equal partners, yet he's constantly making decisions without me."

"He chose the pink t-shirts?"

"You know I did." She swatted his arm. "I mean he chooses the equipment. If he needs something, he buys it without comparison shopping." She pulled her hair out of its band and then replaced it. "He doesn't respect my opinion. I saw a similar shampoo to the brand he insists on for a third of the price, and he refused to even try it." She paced. "'I only use the best.' That's his response to everything." Crossing her arms, she glared at Marc. "Where would Aaron be if I hadn't bought this place and financed the rehab of the shop? My investment makes us equal partners." A tear trailed her cheek. Marc took that as a cue for a hug.

"How long has your brother been a groomer?" Marc held her close, enjoying the smell of lavender and dog products.

"Ten years." Bria sniffed and pulled away. "I know he has the trophies to prove his skill. Still, I want to be heard."

The doorbell interrupted the moment. Bria drew away with pinked cheeks.

"Hey sis," Aaron closed the door behind him and shrugged. "I'm sorry for hiring Drew without asking your opinion. We're a team. I need to remember that."

She nodded and then hugged him. "Perhaps hiring this guy is a good thing?"

"Now we can take in more dogs, which means more money and, wait for it... with an extra groomer that's more time off for us." Aaron grinned.

"Maybe we can both have a life outside this place." He put his arm around her shoulder. "We good?"

She nodded.

"Again, I'm sorry." Aaron headed for the door then turned. "Drew's awesome. He asked if we'd hire his sister as a bather. I told him we'd discuss it. I think we should see how much business Drew generates."

"And we'd have to pay a plumber to repair the other bathing tub."

"True that." Aaron smiled. "I'll make that call when I get home." He waved and left the shop.

Bria reached for Marc's hand. "Thanks for being my sounding board. His apology wouldn't have gone so well. I would've needed to yell at him first."

"My sister is the same when she's mad at me." Marc laughed. "Anytime you need to talk, I'm here."

Bria went to the back room, and Marc opened his laptop to create ideas for the Bowwow Rescue fundraiser. Saturday was the busiest day of the week, so he only got one idea sketched out before Grammie and Tyler arrived with lunch.

Marc took the basket back to the break room. Melancholy filled his heart at the prospect of not seeing Bria every day. Had their time together achieved his goal of more than friendship? Surely, defending her against Mitch counted for something. And being there when Aaron was being unreasonable. Now with the fundraiser, he had more time to build her trust. *God help her see I'm not her vision of all men. Help me be the guy she needs and wants.*

And Father, don't let Tyler's heart get broken if she still doesn't want me.

20

Marc rubbed the bridge of his nose. He moaned in disbelief when he glanced at the time in the corner of his computer screen. Two-thirty. He saved the memes he finished, backed up his computer, and shut down the program. Stretching, he pushed away from his desk and padded toward his bedroom. Sleep deprivation from meeting his client's needs and helping with the fundraiser hammered him. He'd finally finished a gym website and would email the client tomorrow with the link. Tonight, he lingered awake in case Tyler called. This was his first sleepover ever.

He'd not intended to spend most of the evening on Bowwow Rescue. His body craved sleep, but his mind refused to settle. Visions of Bria's smiling face every time he shared his latest addition to the marketing campaign fueled his desire to win her to the girlfriend zone.

The alarm clock blared, pulling him from a dream where Hamilton, Brownie, and an assortment of Bria's clients had bulging muscles as they lifted weights at the Doggie Dynamite Gym. Marc awoke to sunlight across his face.

"What time is it?" He followed the fresh baked smell to the kitchen. "Grammie, is that cinnamon rolls?"

Bria sat on a kitchen chair chatting with his grandmother.

Grateful he wasn't wearing his Superman pjs, he recalled the weightlifting dream. Bria had been a personal trainer in a hot-pink workout suit. She looked every bit as hot now in her jeans and white t-shirt with a giant sunflower on the front.

"What are you doing here?"

"I have Delores' cinnamon roll radar." She smiled and took a bite of the treat. Her look of contentment made him reach for his share.

"Is Tyler still in bed?" Marc reached for the coffee Grammie offered.

"Don't you remember he spent the night with his cousin?" She pulled a plate from the cabinet. "They went to that new Disney movie last night. We're going to meet him at the church's annual picnic later."

"That's right." His sleep deprivation seemed to have squashed the memory of his anxiety over his son's sleepover. "Tyler must be having a great time." If there had been an emotional meltdown, he'd have gotten a call.

Grammie touched his shoulder. "Parents never stop losing sleep over their children."

That's not encouraging. "Well, the upside—more rolls for me." He poured more coffee and added a second roll to the one Grammie had placed on his plate.

"You look exhausted." Bria pushed a wayward lock of hair off his forehead. The warmth of her soft fingers sent a feather-light tingle across his skin. Marc wanted to kiss that hand, but she moved away before he could act.

"I'm tired for sure. After the fundraiser is over next week, I'll catch up on my beauty sleep." The concern in Bria's eyes touched a deep loss in his heart. Other than his grandmother, no other woman had made him feel cared for.

"I stopped by early so we could go over last-minute marketing details before I head to work. My first groom is at ten." Bria pulled out her phone. While they ate, she shared the remainder of the to-do list.

"All my volunteers are amazing. They've stepped up to get stuff done. I've never worked with willing helpers who don't need handholding. Delores, can I bottle your book club's enthusiasm and give it to future volunteers?"

They laughed.

Bria glanced at her list, then gave Marc a sheepish grin. "And we have a problem I hope you can solve."

"What's up?"

"Steve McCall broke his leg in two places. His surgery is today, and he'll be confined to his house for the next few weeks."

"You want me to ask around and see if I can find a replacement?" Marc mentally went down the list of friends and family who might be okay with wearing a kilt.

"I was hoping you'd do it."

"Me? In a skirt? No thank you."

"It's a kilt. A very manly garment." She winked, then took a serious tone. "Besides, we don't have time to come up with a new idea and create a new costume. And I'll not offend Francis Henderson by pulling her Scottish Terrier out of the show."

"Why me?" As much as he didn't like the idea, he knew his resolve was weak when it came to Bria.

"Aaron was willing, but he's needed backstage to handle the dogs. Plus, if his buddy doesn't get over the flu by next Saturday, Aaron will be the Viking." Bria sighed. "The kilt would be a mini-skirt on my brother." Her shudder matched his unpleasant vision of Aaron in the garment.

"Fine. But no wisecracks about my boney knees." Marc licked frosting off his fingers.

"Promise." Bria raised her hand in a Girl Scout salute, then placed a soft kiss on his cheek. "I can breathe again. You're the best."

Before he could kiss her back, she stood.

"I need to fly." She pulled her purse strap over her arm and shoved her phone inside. "See you both later."

Grammie cleared the table. "Why don't you go back to bed? You don't work on Fridays, and we don't need to be at the church until noon."

"Sounds like a plan." Marc rubbed his eyes and yawned. Curled back in bed, his mind flashed scenarios of Bria. He drifted off, reliving her kiss. He could see them together forever... if only she could...

21

At the fundraiser on Saturday, Marc and Tyler, with Brownie in tow, entered the middle school gym that had been transformed into a fashion show setting. Lots of white tulle and twinkling lights were strung overhead with fresh flower bouquets around the room —courtesy of Hank's Florist, one of Marc's clients. He was glad he'd thought of asking them to help out. A potted evergreen shaped like a poodle created the centerpiece to the left of the runway.

"Wow! Daddy this is sooo cool!" Tyler released his hold on Marc's hand and adjusted his cowboy hat. He'd insisted on real cowboy boots with his Woody costume. "Brownie, don't be scared." He leaned down and hugged his furry friend, whose nose pointed heavenward as he took in his new surroundings.

Marc traded Tyler's hand for Brownie's leash and set the pace as they walked toward Aaron.

"Look at those manly legs." Aaron wolf whistled as Marc approached dressed as a Scottish laird. The kilt mortified Marc. The additions of a lacy shirt under his jacket, a matching green plaid hat, and stockings made him grateful it was a one-time thing.

He pushed his embarrassment aside and smiled. "Don't I know it." Marc raised the kilt a bit higher to show off his knees. The shorts he wore underneath peeked from the hem.

"You got it bad if she talked you into wearing that." Aaron guffawed.

"Anything to help the cause." Marc would leave him to decide which cause that was.

"I'm sure once all the other chicks smile at you, she'll come around."

"You think this skirt—kilt is a chick magnet?"

"If it were a bigger size, I'd have worn it—minus the jacket of course." Aaron flexed his muscles.

Marc shook his head. "Easy now, this is a family event."

They chuckled.

"Bria said you'd tell us where to wait."

"I'll take Brownie and get him in costume. You and Tyler can go behind the stage and sit with the other models." Aaron turned to a man dressed in lederhosen with a Saint Bernard at his side.

Marc watched the sportswriter for the newspaper pull on his stockings "Nice outfit, Karl."

Karl shrugged. "My grandmother talked me into this."

"Book club member?" Marc shook his head and grinned.

"Your grandma too?" Karl adjusted the other stocking.

A woman dressed as Cinderella with two Chihuahuas in gray mouse outfits came to Aaron for direction. He took the Saint Bernard and the smaller dogs' leashes. "Follow the Lord of the Dance." He winked as he whisked the dogs away.

Aaron ushered the costumed models to a row of chairs backstage to the left, while Lloyd corralled the dogs into crates on the other side. Aaron and Lloyd would bring out the dogs when it was their turn to walk the runway to avoid any aggression in the ranks.

Marc had met MacGregor, a blue-ribbon Scottish terrier show dog, yesterday during rehearsal. Greggie had been so easy to walk, he'd stayed focus on the task at hand and ignored the other dogs. Brownie, however, had tried to make friends and distracted Tyler. Marc had done his best not to laugh as the enormous Great Dane, Hamilton, quivered and whimpered down the runway.

Now in front of a full house, he waited his turn. The lacy sleeve proved a nice sweat remover. Aaron handed him MacGregor when it was his turn. Marc and Greggie got into position. Bria wore a portable microphone, making it easy for everyone to hear her as she addressed the crowd.

"Saint Bernards are known as the rescue dogs of the Alps. They trudged through snowy passes searching for those who were lost." The dog sprawled out at the end of the runway. "Shiloh loves children and enjoys pulling them in his cart. He is joined by Karl Krutsinger, sports reporter for the Beacon News." Bria passed a treat to Karl, who used it to coax Shiloh off the stage. He had to keep the treat well out of Shiloh's reach which made for a comical exit as Karl resorted to hiding the treat in his hat. Titters of laughter followed the duo. He managed to get off the stage just as Shiloh discovered his hiding place.

On the runway, Greggie took his sweet time reveling in the attention. It allowed Marc to take in the vision of Bria. She wore a long black formal, and her hair waved around her shoulders. She stood at a podium beside the runway and spoke from notecards. The dangling earrings and matching necklace caught the light from the stage and twinkled. If they weren't real diamonds, she made them appear so with her bright smile and beautiful eyes.

Bria focused on the audience.

"MacGregor is a full-sized Scottish terrier. He's won Best of Show and Best of Breed three years running at the American Dog Show."

Marc tuned out her description of his companion and focused on her as he stood at the end of the catwalk.

"MacGregor's handler is the handsome Marc Graham of Graham Advertising." Marc winked at Bria, then bowed to the audience and extended his hand as he'd been instructed the night before. The applause deepened his blush. He turned and escorted his charge off stage. Lloyd took Greggie, so Marc waited in the wings to watch his son.

Tyler adjusted his cowboy hat again. Brownie, decked out as an Indian chief, walked on stage beside him.

"Brownie is a rescue, whose previous owner had lovingly trained him before circumstances forced the owner to surrender his friend to an animal shelter. Unlike shelters, Bowwow Rescue works hard to match each dog with just the right owner." Bria spoke further about their vision as Brownie and Tyler started forward.

The long feather headdress waddled as Brownie headed toward Bria. It drooped to the side as he quickened his pace.

Tyler struggled to hold on to the leash as Brownie's trot became a run. Bria signal for Brownie to stop. He skidded to a halt. Then she signaled. "Go." Brownie panted, then walked calmly off stage, his headdress around his neck. The audience laughed and applauded.

"And that, ladies and gentlemen, is an example of the training we offer in our obedience classes. You'll find the information in your program."

Aaron grabbed Brownie's leash and Tyler took Marc's hand. Aaron escorted Brownie back to his crate.

"Brownie messed up." Tyler's shoulders slumped.

Marc walked his son to a corner away from everyone and lifted his chin.

"Brownie wasn't the only dog to get nervous. And Bria was able to show how well he obeys even when he is afraid. You two gave Miss Bria a chance to talk about her dog obedience classes."

Tyler smiled. "You're right." He hugged his dad. "I was kinda scared when he started running toward Miss Bria. I forgot how to make him stop. I was embarrassed when everyone laughed."

"They weren't laughing at you." Marc pulled him closer. "Maybe Brownie was nervous around MacGregor and some of the other show dogs."

"Other dogs were scared too?"

"Look." Marc pointed toward the stage. Hamilton stood stark still in the center of the stage, wearing huge dragon wings. The giant black Great Dane shivered, causing the wings to shimmer. He refused to move, no matter how much his Viking handler tugged on the leash.

After reciting the history of Great Danes, Bria positioned herself at the end of the catwalk.

"Hamilton. Come."

Her command echoed over the sound system. The Great Dane moved forward. "Come on, sweetie." She pulled a ragged-looking rope from behind her back. Hamilton trotted forward, gave a joyous woof that caused the audience to jump and then laugh. He sat at Bria's feet, his wings wavering while he waited for his toy.

"Hamilton is the largest Great Dane on record. He has a sweet temperament despite his dragon attire."

The dog stared at the toy, oblivious of his surroundings. She handed it to the Great Dane. "Go." He took his toy and scurried back the way he came, the Viking quick stepping at his side. The audience laughed and applauded.

"See, Hamilton was scared too." Marc shoulder hugged his son.

Tyler nodded, and the two found a spot in the last row to watch the rest of the show. The audience's reaction to the parade of dogs impressed Marc. If he'd never met Bria, a fundraiser for a dog rescue would have been the last place he'd have spent a Saturday. Let alone participated in a skirt. *Lord, You sure have a sense of humor.* As Bria gave her closing remarks, he and Tyler went to retrieve Brownie.

Bria came backstage. "Great job, everyone. The newspaper photographer wants a group shot. Then Aaron and I will take the foster dogs out front to see if they might find a forever home. You all can take your own dogs at that point. If we provided the dog a costume, please leave it with Lloyd. Feel free to leave your pets in their crates while enjoying the rest of the festivities if they are uncomfortable with their surroundings."

Marc helped Tyler removed Brownie's headdress.

"Can we go find Grammie?" Tyler kept Brownie close.

"Sure. I need to see Bria." He watched Tyler guide his dog expertly toward Grammie. *My boy's growing up. Father, forgive me for disliking that dog.* Bria walked by.

"What do I do with this kilt?" Marc's neck warmed as she gave him the once over.

"You look like the cover of a historical romance novel. I love it. I would definitely buy that book."

"Me lady, I've come to rescue ye from yer drudgery as ye battle the furry beasties. Let me take ye away from all this." Marc took her hand and kissed it.

"Be still my heart." Bria placed her hand on her chest and laughed. "Too bad you can't wear that on a date." She winked.

"Not on your life." Marc continued holding her hand. The playful glint in her eyes was something new. Maybe the kilt was working for him.

"If you have a change of clothes, you can hand the costume to Lloyd. Otherwise you can wear it home."

"Speaking of dates, when can we plan one? Minus the kilt?" Marc seized the moment like a Highlander fighting for his homeland.

"How about I plan it? I'll call you." Bria stroked the back of his hand, sending shudders up his arm.

"You name the day and time." Marc took her other hand and gazed at her lips.

"Hey, Bria, I could use some help." Aaron struggled with four dogs. Two had managed to get their leashes entangled, and one hid behind his back. "These guys aren't leash-trained."

Bria released Marc's hands and took two dogs. "I'll call you tomorrow." She walked with Aaron toward the adopt-a-dog area. Marc wanted to follow, but she was busy overseeing the evening, and he needed to get out of his kilt and back to Tyler.

Marc joined Tyler and Grammie at the silent auction table. He bid on a Chicago museum package, and Grammie bid on a spa day.

"Daddy, can I bid on that basket?" Tyler pointed to a colorful basket from the Yum Yum Shop overflowing with sweet treats.

Marc pulled Brownie away from a basket full of dog treats and signaled for him to heel. Tonight, he was grateful for all Bria had taught him. Some of the other dogs still waited in their crates until the end of the event. Over the din of voices in the gym, Hamilton's whining could be heard. His owners manned the food booth and had leashed him to a post behind the concession. Marc patted Brownie and tried to reason with Tyler.

"Are you sure you wouldn't rather bid on the dog toy basket? You said Brownie wanted it." Marc hoped Tyler would change his mind.

"Can't I bid on both?" Tyler put on his pouty face and Grammie intervened.

"Tyler, one is enough." Her firm tone brokered no disagreement, and Tyler looked down at Brownie.

"The Yum Yum basket has some dog treats in there, too." Tyler smiled, and Marc added his name to the clipboard with a low bid.

Bria breezed by them several times as she greeted potential donors and adoptive parents. Her beautiful smile would tempt anyone to mortgage their home for her cause. Volunteers passed out goodie bags containing swag any dog lover would appreciate. Brownie kept sniffing the bag in Grammie's hand. She stuffed it in her giant tote and hung the purse from her shoulder. "Not now." Grammie scowled at Brownie as he whined his disappointment.

Marc signaled for him to heel, and he stayed by Marc's side the rest of the evening.

At the end of the silent auction, Marc had lost his bid for the Chicago museum package but won the Yum Yum basket. Apparently, no parents wanted that kind of sugar high for their kids. Grammie came in second on her bid for a spa day and was given a fifty-percent-off coupon.

"Daddy, can I open the basket?" Tyler's whiny tone announced it was time to go home.

"Let's take it home, then you can see what's inside." Marc handed the basket to Grammie, and they headed to the parking lot. Brownie settled in the back seat next to Tyler. They both fell asleep before they drove a block, averting a meltdown over the candy. Marc had forgone saying goodbye to Bria in case Tyler got overly huggy in his tired, whiny state. Bria didn't need that sort of distraction. He'd apologize for his rudeness in a text later.

At home, Marc went online to order a congratulatory bouquet. Looking through the website, he got an idea. If the wall around Bria's heart continued to crumble, now it was time to bring in reinforcements.

22

B ria moaned as she stretched her aching muscles to turn off the alarm. Monday morning. Even with sleeping in and a late start time, exhaustion reigned. She had come home late Saturday night after the fundraiser. She, Aaron, and Lloyd had cleaned up after the dogs and disassembled crates to take back to the shop. Sunday morning, they met the volunteers at the gym and spent the day disassembling their make-shift catwalk, cleaning, and putting the place back in order.

She'd almost added Marc's name to the clean-up crew, but he'd done so much already. As she made her bed, she reviewed all the fun times they'd had together. Opening the gate on her walled heart was both scary and joyful. It was time. She knew exactly what their date would be.

"Play praise mix." Her room filled with music. She glanced at the clock and hurried to the bathroom. She'd spent far too much time daydreaming about a certain Scottish laird.

Rushing out the door with wet hair, her cell phone buzzed. "Where are you!!!!" appeared on her screen from Aaron.

Bria pulled on her seatbelt and texted, "In the car now," and placed her phone on the hands-free stand. The phone rang. She pressed the Blue-tooth button on her steering wheel. "I said I'm on my way." She pulled out of the driveway and headed downtown to the shop.

Woofing echoed over the phone. "Can you grab some donuts?" Aaron sounded out of breath.

"What's going on?"

"An emergency. Hamilton was so happy to get home Saturday night he took longer than usual outside. Jack got worried and went out to look for him. Hamilton had jumped the fence and found a friend in the woods behind their house."

Bria moaned as she pulled into the drive-thru line at Dunkin' Donuts. "He got skunked."

"Yep. Poor guy spent the weekend outside in the shed."

"Why didn't Jack tell us Sunday?"

"He didn't want to add more to our plate." Aaron's volume went up a notch. "Settle down."

"How's it going?"

"I've wrestled him in the bathing room for the last hour. Lloyd came down and gave me a hand." Aaron's voice became distant for a moment.

"Take him to a crate and run the dryer." Aaron's voice became clearer as he appeared to have picked up the phone and taken it off speaker.

Aaron's sigh filled the interior of her car. "Hamilton is super agitated. I need some donuts to go with my coffee. Get two dozen." He hung up.

Bria placed the order, an assortment of filled donuts and pastries. She made sure half a dozen were plain glazed. Lloyd liked to dunk his, and if he saved her from being Aaron's assistant on that mission, he deserved his favorite treat.

She arrived to find Jack ready to take Hamilton home. She laid the boxes on the counter and started the coffee while Aaron collected Jack's payment.

"I owe you guys. You know, we almost took Hamilton home as soon as his turn was up on the runway. Poor guy gets nervous when he's in a new environment. Then he had one of his I-gotta-be-free moments at home." Jack put his credit card back in his wallet, then took out cash and handed it to Aaron and Lloyd. "You guys deserve a generous tip for opening up early for Hamilton." He turned to his giant dog and tugged on the leash. "You get to ride home." Hamilton's bark reverberated in the small space. "He loves riding in the van. The only reason Debbie and I have it is so this big baby can ride in comfort." He opened the shop door for the Great Dane, and the two headed out toward his wife and their waiting vehicle.

Bria poured coffee in mugs.

"They walked here this morning." Lloyd grabbed a plain donut. "They live a good five miles from here. Jack thought Hamilton would be calmer if he got exercise."

"Didn't work." Aaron laughed as he started on his second jelly-filled treat. "Jack didn't want to try and get the skunk scent out of his car, either. Debbie drove the van, and they met for breakfast at the café while we bathed him."

"Those two do everything together." Bria sighed. "They hold hands everywhere they go."

"When I finally find the woman of my dreams, I want that. Growing old together, still holding hands and enjoying each other's company." Aaron nodded toward the window.

"I had no idea you dreamed about women. I assumed it was weightlifting and football." Bria teased.

"There's a lot you don't know about me." Aaron refilled his coffee cup as the doorbell rang.

"Flowers for..." The delivery man looked at the tag on the bouquet. "Bria Willis."

She signed for the flowers and placed the vase of red roses on the counter. "There's no name."

"It has to be Marc." Aaron picked up the ringing phone. "Did you get the final tally for the dog show?"

Bria smelled the red roses before placing the vase on the counter. "We raised enough money to not only keep BowWow Rescue going for two years, but we can hire a few people to help Clara. That means we have more opportunities to help more dogs and the volunteers can be overseen and scheduled more effectively. I can't wait." She needed to let Marc know about their success—thanks to him—and to thank him for the flowers.

"Wow! That's fantastic, not only do you get more time for yourself now that we hired Drew, but BowWow Rescue should run smoother and its acting president won't have to put in so many extra hours."

"Once we hire the extra help, I hope to be back to bathing a few times a week."

"Don't fill up too much of your free time, or your new boyfriend might get jealous of the dogs." Aaron wagged his eyebrows as he grabbed another donut.

Bria's blush made Aaron grin. She didn't bother to punch his arm, instead she grabbed a donut and headed to the back room where she could text her new boyfriend in private.

New boyfriend... she liked how that sounded.

∾

MORE MYSTERY DELIVERIES arrived throughout the week. A stuffed Scottie dog, a model train, a hiking canteen, and two more bouquets of flowers joined the roses on the counter. Now it was Friday, and Bria kept peeking out from the grooming room every time the doorbell rang.

"Let me guess— no Marc so far?" Aaron leaned over the half-door and smirked.

"He hasn't called." She glared at Aaron, then scanned her messages. "His texts are short." Bria chewed her lower lip. "What if he's done his good deeds, and now we're done? He didn't even call when I thanked him for all he did to make the fundraiser a success."

"Didn't you say he texted he had a lot of work to catch up on?" Aaron would defend him. Typical guy.

Her phone binged and her heart warmed, forgetting her worry for the moment. "Look, he sent another dog video." She turned the phone to Aaron. She hadn't been this anxious about hearing from a guy since her eighth-grade crush dumped her.

"See, you're on his mind."

"This morning, he sent a photo of Tyler and Brownie playing in the park." She scrolled through the messages and showed her brother.

"Told ya." Aaron winked and disappeared into the back room.

She was at the front desk on the phone making an appointment when lunch was delivered. The smell of chicken wings made her stomach growl. They'd adopted lunch break as a regular part of their schedule. Even closing the shop for an hour so they could all eat. Another thoughtful thing Marc had done to change her life. Aaron paid the delivery guy as the mail carrier dropped off a package for her.

"I'll put out lunch while you open that." Aaron nodded with his chin, then took the food to the break room where Lloyd joined him. Bria tore open the packing box. A Mouse Maze action figure stared up at her with a note inside. "Still waiting for our do-over date."

Bria looked at her gifts, embarrassed she had forgotten to confirm their date. No wonder he hadn't called her. He must think she ghosted him. "Now all the gifts make sense."

The roses were now fully open. Red roses represented love. Could Marc be hinting his feelings of more than friendship? Then he sent gifts connected to their memories together, starting with the dog show with the stuffed Scottie dog. The train for their Chicago trip, the canteen for their hike, and the other floral bouquets—exact replicas of the ones he'd given her while they were dating. Now the mouse figurine going back to their first non-date at Mouse Maze

Bria put the mouse at the end of the line of gifts and sent Marc a text. "Dinner at my house Sunday afternoon."

The phone pinged. "I'll be there."

Bria smiled at the smiley-heart emoji, then clasped the phone to her chest, and went to find her brother.

23

Marc took one last look in the mirror. Grammie had taken Tyler and Brownie to visit his cousins. The chiming of the mantle clock reminded Marc he needed to get moving. He grabbed the bouquet of daisies, then locked the door.

The short walk to Bria's home wasn't the cause of the perspiration forming on his neck. He'd been super busy since the fundraiser finishing up projects for other clients he'd set aside to meet Bria's need. He could have taken some time to meet Bria for lunch or actually call rather than text. His foolish insecurity had kept him from moving forward. She'd said she would call him about their next date. Would she have remembered if he hadn't added the note to her last gift? Was this a pity date? Pushing that thought from his mind he enjoyed the prospect of spending time with her today. The adrenaline running in his veins sent a buzz of anticipation through him.

He had no idea she could cook. Inviting him for dinner in her home was a big deal. Did she understand the message behind the gifts? It was corny, and he'd almost stopped with the roses.

But he always followed through with things, even if the results went south. His thoughts went to the many ways his relationship with Janet had soured. *Please, Lord, don't let things sour this time.*

Bria wasn't Janet by any stretch of the imagination.

Aaron opened the door. "Welcome to Chez Willis. Let me take those flowers."

Marc stepped in but held the flowers close. "Where's Bria? And why are you here?"

"Bria is making herself beautiful, and I am the cook." Aaron shut the door. "You really didn't think she knew how, did you?" Aaron chuckled.

"I do know how to cook." Bria strolled down the hall, taking his breath away in a royal blue sheath dress and silver stilettos. Her hair was in a French braid, and large silver hoops that matched her necklace and bracelets adorned her ears.

"I'm underdressed." Marc found his voice.

She smiled and took the flowers. "You spoil me." She kissed his cheek, then moved away.

"Dinner is ready, take your seats." Aaron pointed to a table for two set up in the living room. He took the flowers from Bria and headed back to the kitchen.

Her couch and over-stuffed chair had been pushed to the side. A blue candle complimented the pattern on the place settings. A coffee cup and a stemmed goblet sat at each place, and a cloth napkin shaped like an origami bird graced the middle of the plates.

"Did you do all this?" Marc sat at the table.

"All but the napkin folding. Aaron watched a YouTube tutorial." Bria laughed and reached for his hand. "I wanted to recreate our special date in Chicago, minus the paparazzi." She rubbed her thumb over his palm, spreading warmth up his arm. Then she grabbed the napkin and flipped it, dissolving the bird into flat linen. "Aaron is a fantastic cook. I asked him to make something special."

"How'd you talk him into it?" Marc suspected her brother was an unofficial chaperone.

Aaron placed soup in front of them. "She promised I could watch the Cubs game on her giant screen TV. The game starts in an hour, so let's move it along." He wiggled his eyebrows and strolled back to the kitchen. The music filling the room drowned out Aaron's humming as he cooked.

Aaron served five courses and gave them ample time between each to enjoy the meal and light conversation. By the time the crème-Brule arrived for dessert, the connection Bria had pulled the plug on now sparked to life.

"Well, sis." Aaron took away their empty dessert plates. "I'll turn on the dishwasher, but this mess is on you. The game starts in five minutes."

Aaron disappeared into the den, and the sound of the ball game drifted from the room.

"Let's take our coffee out to the patio." Bria took her cup and Marc followed. The patio table held his bouquet, and soft music streamed from speakers near the back door. The sun sank lower in the sky. A breeze cooled the otherwise muggy air.

"This is great." Time alone with her was an answered prayer. Now he needed to take advantage of this blessing. He reached across the table and took her hand. He kissed her palm and folded her fingers over to seal it in place. "You know I can't be your friend anymore."

BRIA'S HEART froze with his words. His eyes held hers, their warmth belying his statement.

"I can't be just a friend. I'm in love with you and if you don't feel the same I...."

"I do." Bria rose from her chair, her hand still in his. He joined her. "I love you too."

He caressed her face. His lips moistened her forehead, then her cheeks, and at last found her lips. His confession restated in delicious tingles with his kiss. Then he pulled her to him, she melted into his embrace. Their kiss intensified until a moan rose from Marc.

He released her and stepped back. Passion smoldered in his eyes. "I suppose it's safe to say we are a couple again."

"Very safe." Bria stepped closer. "I've never felt this safe before. You've done your best to show me you care, and I can trust you. That's hard for me to do, but not with you. I know you will never hurt me or make me change into something I'm not."

"Never." Marc ran his hands down her bare arms, bringing more waves of warm tingles. She pressed herself close to him and initiated a kiss. He returned it, but with less ardor than before. Gently, he pushed her away and gazed into her eyes. "If I ever make you feel like you're losing yourself, tell me."

"You won't, I'm confident you're not that kind of man. I chose to become Brittany, but I let Mitchell define who that was." Bria sat in the patio chair, placing some distance between them. Marc took the other chair again. "She would never have allowed herself to be compromised. Brittany had strong faith and let others know it. My insecurity and lack of faith led me down the path to a bad relationship." She didn't look at him, instead, Bria sipped her now tepid coffee, gathering her courage.

"I need to tell you something." She took a deep breath. "I was pregnant with Mitch's child. We had an argument, and I fell down the stairs. It caused a miscarriage." She turned away from him and stared at the horizon.

"I suspected as much by your comments to Mitch when he came to the shop." His fingers entwined with hers across the table.

"I'm not pure." Tears blurred her vision. "Coming home, and with the support of my family, I found my true self. I know God has forgiven my past and made me new."

She disengaged her hand from his. The distance made it easier to continue.

"I did a lot of things I'm not proud of during those years. But I tried to maintain my moral standard. It wasn't my idea to have sex." She stared above his head, not wanting to see his reaction. "The short version of it is that he spiked my drink. Then he blamed me when he drove drunk and wrecked my car taking me home."

"I understand date-rape drugs numb your mind." Gentleness covered his words.

She nodded as shame draped across her shoulders. "I didn't dispute the DUI. I was so emotionally messed up during that time in my life. I let Mitch do my thinking." She put her hands in her lap. A breeze pulled tendrils of hair from her braid into her face, and she pushed them out of her eyes. "Once I discovered I was pregnant, I thought perhaps...." She leaned forward. Her voice cracked. "It horrified Mitch at first when he found out about the baby."

Marc's jaw flexed, but he remained silent.

"Then he promised to take care of us. I moved in with him." Bria licked her lips. "I'd held on to some insane notion he'd come to love me. Up until he slammed me against the wall and caused me to fall down the stairs during another of our arguments. I lost the baby that night." She placed her hand on the table palm up. "Are you sure you want to get involved with me?"

He held on tight to her hand. "I drank and was a party guy for the first year I was married to Janet. Are you sure you can live with that?" Marc's unexpected answer washed over like cold water on a burn. Silence sat between them for a few minutes.

"I never called the police," she said. "I was so ashamed of who'd I'd become. Losing the baby hurt so much. It felt like God was punishing me for pursuing something out of His will for me."

Marc ran his thumb over her knuckles, and the action gave her courage to continue.

"I took a good look at myself in the hospital's bathroom mirror. The reflection wasn't pretty. I checked myself out before Mitch came to pick me up. Then I had my lawyer escort me home, and I packed a bag and told him to sell Brittany's things. I've never looked back."

"I understand. Becoming a dad woke me up and showed me how selfish my marriage had been. I tried to change, and fix our broken family. But Janet decided the best way to fix it was to divorce me and take Tyler for the child support." He sighed and continued rubbing her knuckles. "I felt betrayed and worthless." His sapphire eyes darkened for a moment.

"Then she died and left me a single dad." He loosened his grip. "Tyler and I were almost strangers because I'd worked so much. I was too ashamed to ask for help at first. But when all my worldly goods went to pay for a funeral, medical bills, and legal fees, I got a wake-up call to swallow my pride and come home. The therapist and Grammie have helped me learn to be a good father. I like myself better away from the stress of the corporate world."

Bria smiled at the sensitive man across from her. "I like the man you've become." Had she not taken the grieving detour of giving Brittany's memory value, she might have met him sooner. "You're a great dad."

"That means a lot." Marc smiled and leaned toward her. She drew closer over the table. He stroked her cheek. "You're good for Tyler. He's in love with you, too."

"You know, if he were twenty years older, I would dump you for him." Bria's remark brought a laugh from Marc that lasted until he could barely breathe.

"Are you all right?"

Marc took a cleansing breath. "Yes. I've never laughed as much in my life. You make me happy." He kissed her fingers.

"Hey, love birds. The game is over, and I got to fly." Aaron's presence filled the back door. He eyed the couple with his brotherly, protective stare. Marc blushed.

"I need to get home before Tyler arrives or he'll worry where I am." Marc turned to Bria. "I didn't tell him about our date, just in case we... we weren't on the same page. Sorry, I didn't have more faith in us." He pressed

a chaste kiss to her mouth. "I'll call you later." Then he followed Aaron out
the door.

Bria watched from the window as Aaron pulled out of the driveway and
Marc walked home. The day had been perfect, He'd been everything she
needed, Bria had asked Aaron to interrupt them after he watched the
game. She was afraid of where things might go if they were alone in her
house. And if she got uncomfortable, Aaron would rescue her. Marc
proved to her he wasn't the kind of guy to take advantage or make a scene
when he clearly wanted to stay. His gallantry warmed her, pushing the
lonely feeling he evoked when the door closed to the background.

Before she could change into leisure clothes to put her living room in
order, the phone rang. She checked the caller ID.

"Marc, how nice of you to call." Her chuckle matched his on the other
end. She slipped out of her heels and settled in the overstuffed chair,
tucking her feet under her. She cradled the cell phone close, hanging on
his every word.

24

Six weeks later.

Bria grabbed another bottle of water and gulped it at the counter. She pushed strands of hair out of her eyes as she went over their schedule on the computer.

Since the dog show, Doggie Designer Duo had appointments booked until Christmas. The poodle-shaped evergreen sat out in front of the store as a thank you for the additional business the event had given the florist. She suspected no one else would want a dog-shaped bush and the expense of keeping it trimmed.

"Aaron, I thought I had three more grooms this afternoon."

Her brother, busy cutting bandanas from Halloween fabric, gave her a wink. *What is he up to?*

Drew came from the back room, his Captain America t-shirt drenched. "Who decided I should bathe Hamilton?"

"Lloyd had an appointment with a VA doctor." Aaron put away his scissors. "You're the new guy, you gotta learn the ropes."

"Hire Meghan and then she'll be the new guy." Drew mentioned it at every opportunity.

"Maybe we'll give her a chance over the holidays." Bria threw her empty bottle in the trash. "Our schedule should be crazy insane."

"Tell Meghan she can start in two weeks." Aaron looked to Bria for confirmation. "It'll give her time to get use to things before it starts raining dogs in here."

Bria sighed. She usually loved the busy schedules, but less time with Marc and Tyler was taking its toll. She daydreamed about her blond beau and his quirky child. And her night dreams were full of walks in the woods and lots of warm kisses from her Scottish laird. She went to the computer and clicked again to the appointment calendar. "What happened to my three appointments?"

Aaron shrugged. "Didn't I tell you? They rescheduled for next week."

"Weird." Bria noticed the warmth creeping up Aaron's collar. "What's going on?"

"I thought you deserved a break today." Aaron patted her arm. "Why not clean up a bit before you go home?"

"You sound like Mom." Bria laughed and went to the bathroom to wash up and comb her hair.

The doorbell chimed as she exited the bathroom. Aaron and Drew had disappeared. Marc and Brownie entered. A nervous look flitted across Marc's face for a moment. When she came forward, his smile sent her heart soaring. She took his hand.

"What are you doing here? It's not time for Brownie to be groomed." She looked down at the already well-groomed mutt. "What's that around his neck?"

Marc reached for her other hand and drew her close. "Brownie is why we're together. If he hadn't been so afraid of grooming shops, and I hadn't been so ignorant of dog behavior, you and I wouldn't have met. I thought it was only fair to have him as my wingman—dog today."

Marc released her hands and squatted next to Brownie, taking the black satin bag hanging from his collar and removing a velvet ring box. Bria gasped. The doorbell rang, but her focus remained on Marc. He took her hand and got on one knee. "Will you marry me?"

"And be my mom?" Tyler came up next to her, then knelt beside his father. Bria looked up to see Delores and her parents. Aaron and Drew stood grinning from the backroom doorway.

She looked at Marc through a teary blur. "Yes, I'll marry you." Then she turned to Tyler. "And be your mom."

Marc's kiss lingered as long as it could, with Tyler hugging them. Grammie took pictures while Aaron hooted, and the others applauded. Her mom hugged them both and her father, wiping a tear off his cheek, shook Marc's hand.

"Treat her right." Her father placed her hand in Marc's.

"Always, sir." Marc's kiss sealed that promise. His embrace assured Bria. Trusting this sweet man had become so easy.

Bria pointed at Aaron, grinned, and shook her head. "I knew you were up to something." Bria laid her head on Marc's shoulder. "But this time I'm glad."

Marc kissed her again and again. "If not for your brother, we'd never gotten to this place. He wouldn't let me give up."

Bria cuddled between her two loves and smiled at the others. "I was more than surprised. And so happy you're all here."

Brownie woofed. Bria broke from the others and hugged him. "My own personal cupid." He licked her face, and the group laughed.

EPILOGUE

Bria breathed a sigh as the spring sunshine broke through the cloudy sky. "I'm so relieved." Bria leaned near her mom as they posed for pre-wedding photos. "No rain." She held her bouquet close to her waist, trying to find her modeling poise to keep her hands from shaking.

The photographer had been suggesting poses and snapping away for thirty minutes. Bria's phobia of the paparazzi didn't raise its ugly head even once. Marc had the photographer sign a waiver stating she would not use their wedding photos for advertising. He'd done the same with the videographer.

"You look so beautiful, Bria." Chloe, her baby sister, looked lovely in a mint green bridesmaid gown. Fresh from art school, she'd arrived early enough to transform the tent into a fairyland of flowers and lights.

"I'm so happy you're here with me. I've missed you." Bria hugged her, risking wrinkling her dress.

"I've missed you and the rest of our crazy family." Chloe helped Bria straighten her veil. "The simple lines in your dress make you look angelic."

Bria laughed and shoulder-hugged her sister. "Even though I know Marc is my soulmate I'm still nervous."

"It makes you look lovelier." Chloe handed her the bouquet. Her mother smoothed her train. Having her mother as her matron of honor and Chloe at her side was a perfect complement to Marc's witnesses. Aaron and Tyler stood at the front of the tent. Bria stood at the back of the line as Delores, acting as flower-grandmother, guided Brownie the ring bearer up the aisle. Marc's sister and her children formed the string quartet. Bria watched the wedding party walk toward Marc's uncle, their officiant.

Her father's eyes moistened as they walked down the aisle. He lifted her veil and kissed her cheek. "God answered our prayers when He brought Marc to you." He waited for the question.

"Who gives this woman?"

"Her mother and I do," choked from his lips. He patted her hand, and for a second time placed it in Marc's. He stepped away, leaving her to face the beginning of a wonderful future.

Marc leaned in. "Soon you'll be mine forever."

Once they were pronounced man and wife, Tyler came forward. "I promise to love you as my mommy forever and ever." He hugged her hard. She kissed his cheek, and Brownie barked.

MARC'S FACE hurt from smiling as he kept his bride beside him. The last of the wedding guests left as they stood near the opening of the tent, shaking hands. "I can't believe you're mine."

She stroked his cheek and left a lingering kiss on his lips. "I hope that helps you never forget."

"You might have to remind me several more times." Marc felt a tug on his jacket.

"Daddy, when do we go to the zoo?" Tyler's fatigue echoed in his words.

"After we get back from our honeymoon." Marc and Bria kissed the boy, and Grammie took his hand.

"Let's take Brownie home so he can rest. Then you can plan which animals you want to see when your dad and mom return."

They headed toward her Mustang. Brownie stopped to nibble at crumbs of food near the trash can.

"How do you like being called Mom?" Marc's blue eyes sparkled with joy.

Bria grinned. "Wonderful. But right now, I think I love the sound of 'wife' best of all."

THANK YOU FOR READING! If you enjoyed, be sure to leave a review on Amazon and/or Goodreads so others can find it, too!

ACKNOWLEDGMENTS

First and foremost, I want to thank Jesus for the gift of words. Without His grace, I wouldn't be able to stay on task to finish my novels. I am so grateful to my husband of 50 years for his support. Thank you, Charley, for reading every word and helping me make it better, for putting up with my verbal walk through of my plots without complaint. And for cooking meals and doing laundry, so I have time to get this out into the world.

Thank you, Word Weavers and ACFW critique partners. Your input was so instrumental in making things better as I created this work of fiction. And dog groomer children. David and Nicole, and their groomer friends who shared fun stories that were added to this book.

PRAISE FOR CINDY ERVIN HUFF

Ms. Huff continues to charm her readers in her latest contemporary romance, *Loving the Dog Groomer*. Believable characters dealing with scars from past relationships will draw readers into the story. This contemporary romance intertwined with plenty of doggie challenges will make pet lovers swoon! An enjoyable read!

~ Sandra Merville Hart, Award-winning Author of Spies of the Civil War series and Second Chances series

~

What's not to love about a romance set in motion by a big hairy dog? Cindy Huff brings her romantic touch to contemporary audiences with this sweet, small-town furry love story."
   ~ Karin Beery, author of hopeful fiction with a healthy dose of romance

~

Cindy Ervin Huff has a winner with "Loving the Dog Groomer". You name it, this story has it: animal behavior, raising a traumatized child, single parenting, addictions and abuse, death of a loved one, homelessness, PTSD, lack of trust, poor choices, shame, and more. Yet the author weaves each issue into a seamless story of learning to trust God—and others—again. If you enjoy dogs, children, faith, and romance, you're sure to love this story as I did. Can't wait to see what Ms. Huff brings for an encore in her next book.
   ~ Donna Schlachter, author of cozy and historical mysteries.

THE DOG GROOMER'S SOULMATE IS COMING SOON

Keep reading for a free preview of the next book.

THE DOG GROOMER'S SOULMATE
CHAPTER 1

"Aaron." The hum of the busy coffee shop almost drowned out the barista.

Aaron Willis strode toward the counter for his order. A body collided with him, and hot liquid poured down over him. "Ahh!"

His chest was on fire. He clawed at the front of his shirt to separate the heat from his chest. Without a thought, he whipped off his shirt. Then took the dry part and wiped the coffee off his chest.

A woman with auburn hair stood inches from him, trying to dab his chest with napkins. Aaron grabbed her hand as a floral scent surrounded him. She looked up at him with anxious hazel eyes.

"Please stop." His gruff tone caused her to step back.

"I'm so sorry. Is it bad?" Her soulful concern calmed him.

Aaron softened his voice and offered a weak smile.. "It's Okay. I'll be fine."

He stepped to the barista, paid for his food, and headed out. Before he could reach the door, he noticed phones focused on him.

"Great, just great," he muttered under his breath. Someone would have it on their social media in the next ten seconds. What was wrong with people? He kept his face forward as he headed for his truck.

"Aaron." Brad Morgan, his best friend since high school, followed him out of the cafe. "Well, well, Adonis. You already have 50 likes, and a few women want your number."

"I doubt that." Aaron growled as he escaped to his SUV.

He threw his wet T-shirt on the floor of the front passenger side. Coffee puddled around it. "Man, now I have to have the car interior detailed."

"Hey, bro, it's no big thing. It's not like you're fat anymore."

"Really, Brad?" Aaron sighed. He sorted through a box in the backseat full of T-shirts from his shop. He gave them away at events. Finding a triple X sleeveless, he pulled it over his head, hissing as it rested on his scorched chest.

"Need me to take you to the ER." All teasing gone from his voice.

"Nah. You still got that first aid kit in your car?" Aaron pulled up the shirt to reveal the red skin starting to blister.

"Looks like a mild second-degree burn. I don't have the right size bandage, but we'll work it out." Brad scanned the parking lot. "But let's head to the park. It's kinda weird to mess with your burn out here. One of those phone filming freaks might make that part two." Brad headed for his car. "Meet you there."

Aaron followed his friend to a nearby park. Brad, being an EMT, meant he didn't waste hours at the ER waiting to be seen. Once at the park, they settled at an empty picnic table.

Soon, Aaron had salve on his burn covered with an oversized bandage. Brad looped it over his shoulder and pieces of the gauze sat near his neck.

"It looks worse than it is with this enormous bandage. But better than going to work without treating it. Pouring my bottle of ice water over it took out a lot of the heat." Brad sat across from him at a picnic table. "Stop at the fire station after work and I'll redo this with a smaller bandage. In a few days, you won't need one."

Aaron opened his bag and retrieved his breakfast sandwich. "I have a second if you want it."

"Sure." Brad stared at his friend. "What's going on with you? Granted, you were scalded, but normally you're not short with people. You didn't get the title 'Aaron the kind' for nothing."

"Ha, ha. You and your medieval titles. No one calls me that." Aaron sipped his now tepid coffee. "She didn't deserve that. I had two hours of sleep last night and was frozen to the bone by the time I got home this morning."

"You volunteered to sleep in a cardboard box with the youth group again?" Brad shook his head. "There is always that magic word, no. I use it all the time. No way was I spending my Friday night babysitting a bunch of teens."

"Yeah, I should learn that word. I like the teens, but I'm tired of being the go-to guy to chaperone. Can't their parents sleep in cardboard boxes with their own kids?" Aaron huffed. "One good thing, those twenty kids left with a different attitude about their lives and a desire to help those on the streets."

"Didn't it rain last night?"

"A thunderstorm melted my box like it was made of ice cream. When I got home, I stood in the hot shower until the water started to cool." Aaron pitched his trash bag into the can several feet away. It tottered on the edge before falling into the can." He rose and smiled at Brad. "Score." He fished out his car keys. "Maybe that's a sign."

"You should join a basketball team?" Brad laughed as he stepped toward the can and dropped in the sandwich wrapper.

"A sign the rest of the day might be better. It's gotta improve from how it started with little sleep and coffee burns on my chest."

"Aaron, don't let video being out there bother you. Be your cool, nothing-bothers-me self and everyone will forget about it."

"I'm not cool. I'm humiliated."

"Don't be. You've some majorly cool tats, and a body that women would love to touch."

"What is wrong with you, man? Have you been watching those steamy romance movies with your sisters again?"

"I will neither confirm nor deny it." Brad grinned, then frowned. "Hey, you haven't mentioned to anyone about my sisters' guilty pleasure?"

"Why would I?" Aaron shook his head. "Brad, when are you going to focus on real women, and not those Barbie dolls in those movies?"

"When you find someone." Brad opened his car door. "That cute chick who spilled coffee on you might be a place to start."

"If Bria or Chloe heard you refer to a woman as a chick, you'd find a stiletto coming toward your head."

"True. I'm just saying you need to find other pastimes than babysitting teens, fantasy football and guarding your sisters from your best friend."

"I don't do that anymore. Bria's married and Chloe is living in Indianapolis. Far from my creepy friend."

"So, I followed Chloe around when we were in high school. Not my best moment. I was trying to work up the nerve to ask her to prom."

"After I told you my sisters were off limits."

"Brittany had already turned me down and Bria had her face in her books." Brad laughed. "Yeah, I tried to ask them out just to irritate you." Brad had a major crush on Brittany even after she was diagnosis with cancer. Her death hit him as hard as it did Aaron. He'd have been fine with her going to prom with him. He sighed and

"Grow up, bro. We're both thirty-three with no prospects."

"True, but we both have good jobs, which are more than most of the other guys in our fantasy football league can say." Brad slipped into his vehicle and rolled down the window. "Call me and we can go bowling or something."

As Aaron drove to work, he sent up a prayer. *Lord, forgive my attitude this morning. But man, I am just so tired of being the guy everybody relies on for help. Look, I don't mind helping. Really, I don't... It's just feels like life is passing me by.*

For a moment, loneliness overwhelmed him. The words he said to Brad circled in his head. He was thirty-three with no prospects. Not even anyone he was interested in. Unless you count the crazy lady who spilled coffee on him. She'd asked how he was and tried to help him. As awkward as the attempt was, he appreciated her concern.

Aaron groaned. He'd been such a jerk. But hey, scalding coffee would make anyone ornery. He headed toward another heavy schedule of dog grooms.

***

Cassie Quinn watched the bare-chested man leave the coffee shop. Mortification covered her face. The manager she'd just interviewed with watched the whole scene. He scowled at her. Well, this job was iffy anyway. He'd already ask the perfunctory do you think you can be a Barista with your artificial arm. Then she squeezed the coffee cup too hard while trying to walk and pull her backpack on, thus turning the cup into a pour spout. Could her day get any worse?

She hefted her backpack over her artificial arm and then over her left arm and secured it before leaving the café.

Her phone buzzed. Pulling it from her skirt pocket, she sighed. "Hey, Callie."

"How's your interviews going so far?"

"On a scale from one to ten, I'd say a negative three."

She could hear Callie speaking with her assistant before she returned to the phone. "I'm sure they'll get better." Her sister's half-hearted encouragement irritated her.

"You do know the state requires employees to interview any disabled vet who applies for a job. Most have no intention of hiring me. The last interview seemed promising until I spilled my scalding coffee on a customer." She filled her sister in. "I kinda squeezed the entire content on the man. When he whipped off his shirt..."

"He took off his shirt." Callie chuckled, bringing heat to Cassie's face. She headed toward her mustang.

"Yeah, I soaked him in scalding liquid." Trying to explain how she tried to help the guy sent her sister into peels of laughter. "Thanks for your sympathetic ear. The guy could be scarred for life." She pulled open her car door, slid inside, and placed her phone on the hands-free caddy.

"Sorry. I shouldn't laugh, but I saw the video on social media just before you called. It had a million views already. I couldn't tell who the woman was. Only her left hand on his chest. The guy was handsome and hot."

"I didn't notice. I was too embarrassed. If I'd sat my coffee on a table, then put on my backpack, nothing would have happened. I keep forgetting how sensitive the mechanism is on my arm." She felt like a cyborg every time she broke something. She'd not mastered the motor skills for delicate maneuvers. "I'm so done with interviews." And people gawking at her arm with doubtful looks at her ability to do the job.

"I gotta go. The internet at my apartment is awful, so I need to check if I got any more interviews in my email."

"Sure. I'll see you at the folks' this weekend. And sis, you know you don't have to work. Why stress yourself out?" Before Cassie could explain her reason again, she'd hung up.

***

By the time Cassie left the library, she was calmer and a little hopeful. She'd filled out three more applications and secured an interview that afternoon.

She parked in front of Doggie Designer Duo. Cassie laughed at the large pink sign with a poodle under a hair dryer. This could be a fun place to work or not. She'd have to convince them she could do whatever was required of her.

Front office work was small potatoes, as Grandpa liked to call things that were so easy you could do them with your eyes closed. She'd managed the general's schedule, and every other aspect of her life, until that fateful day that ended her career.

Her parents insisted she didn't need to work because she collected military disability. But boredom only brought on more anxiety and nightmares of the accident that took her forearm and General Byrd.

The doorbell tinkled as she entered. A stunning woman with her long, dark hair in a ponytail greeted her with a warm smile. "How may I help you? "

"I'm here about the office manager's job." Cassie offered a friendly smile, tamping down her nervousness. After running the general's office for years, why did she feel like a teenager at her first job interview? This was her 10th interview and hopefully her last. Her confidence couldn't take much more.

"That's wonderful. I'm Bria Graham. You filled out your application online. Can you wait a minute while I print it out?"

"Sure." She took a seat in one of the plastic chairs in the lobby. Dogs barked from the backroom, nearly drowning out the lobby music playing overhead. There were five large trophies on a top shelf behind the counter and shelves of grooming products and even dog food for sale. She noted a few chew toys and pamphlets on dog care. The large front window had been tinted, so the light came in but not the glare. Before her nerves went into overdrive, Bria reappeared.

"That online application is an auto system my husband set up. Makes our life a bit easier. Your interview goes on my schedule, so I don't forget." She pointed to a door to her left. "Come to my office. I'll grab my brother and be right with you."

Cassie took a seat in front of a cluttered desk in what looked like a storage room. The shelves were lined with shampoos and other dog grooming products. A large shop vac, industrial wringer bucket and mop, along with a broom resting in a corner. A shelf of towels sat above a washer and dryer. Both were on and by the sound of them had seen better days. The dryer buzzer went off as Bria entered the room.

"Aaron will be with us shortly." Bria walked to the desk, a copy of Cassie's resume in hand. "He has to call a dad to pick up Ralphie."

Bria giggled. "I can see by that look you don't own a dog. We refer to all owners as parents. Ralphie's owner wants a call when we are done, to pick him up right away. While others drop their pets off in the morning and don't return until after work."

Cassie nodded, straightened her spine, and pulled together all her military poise.

"I read over your resume last night. I must say I'm very impressed." Bria set the resume in front of her on the desk. "I have one question for you. Why would you work at a dog grooming salon with all your experience? You could write your own job ticket."

A knock interrupted them. And the man she'd spilled coffee on appeared in the door. He wore a sleeveless pink T-shirt that matched the sign. His muscular physique could pull it off. A dry lump sat in her throat as warmth covered her face. He stepped in without smiling. Not a good sign. Her palm sweated, and she glided her hand down her slacks as she crossed her legs and attempted to wipe off the dampness discreetly.

"Cassie, this is my brother, Aaron Willis. Aaron, this is Cassandra Quinn. She's here about the front desk job. Did you get a chance to read her resume last night?"

"No. I was sleeping in the cardboard box." Aaron offered a weak smile.

"My brother chaperoned the teens from the church youth group."

"Yeah, we slept in cardboard boxes so they could experience homelessness." Aaron turned to Cassie. "I need to apologize to you for being so grumpy at the coffee shop. A lack of sleep is the only excuse I have." A piece of gauze peeked out the top of his t-shirt and when he moved, she could see a large bandage under his arms.

Cassie stared at him for a moment. She had expected him to glower, not to be so kind. "I should apologize. I spilled my coffee all over you. Are you alright?"

"I'll survive. Don't worry about it." Aaron offered a shrug.

"Ah, you're the one in that video where Aaron is ripping off his shirt." Bria chuckled while Aaron moaned.

"Brad assured me it was no big deal. But people seem to find inappropriate things funny. Don't worry about it, Cassie, tight?"

She nodded, but before she could apologize again, Aaron shook her hand.

"Let's get this done."

Bria picked up her resume. "Her qualifications are outstanding. She's a former Air Force attaché to a general. Sounds so exciting. Cassie spent ten years in the service doing all sorts of clerical and other interesting stuff. I just asked her, with all her qualifications, why she wanted to work at a dog salon."

"I'd like to know the answer to that." Aaron took the seat beside her in front of the desk.

Both siblings sat waiting for her response. Pleading her case based on her abilities hadn't done much in previous interviews. Her mother's reminder to always be honest came to the forefront of her thoughts.

"No one will hire me because I only have one arm." Cassie raised her right prosthetic. Both of them watched as she flexed the fingers, moved the wrist, bent the elbow, then placed it on her lap.

"Amazing." Aaron smiled. "I'm impressed with whoever made your prosthetic. The freckles on your arm matched the ones on the rest of you."

Bria glared at her brother, seeming to be irritated at his remark. Then she nodded her way. "Are you left-handed?"

"I am now." Cassie sighed, her face warming. "I spent two years in therapy learning how to do things left-handed and master my prosthetic, so my movements were natural. But if this is a problem for you, I understand."

"It's not a problem for us if you can run the front office, we really don't care." Bria looked to her brother for confirmation.

"Helping with grooming is not in your job description. But an occasional helping hand when there is only one of us back there and the dog needs to be held still while we clip nails can happen."

"That would be rare because we always have at least two of us here." Bria added.

Aaron offered a smile. "If you can handle nervous dogs and diva dog owners, I think you're in."

"I agree." Bria laid the resume on the table and folded her arms on the desk.

"Seriously?" Cassie's voice cracked before she pulled herself together. "I assume you'll do a background check and a few other things, right?"

"I think your resume speaks for itself. Can you start Monday?" Bria rose from the desk.

"Yes." Relief covered her like a shawl. Having a daily routine would go a long way toward warding off nightmares.

Bria glanced at her watch. "I have an appointment in five minutes. Aaron, could you show her around?"

"Sure." He gestured toward the door, and they all filed out.

"This way." Aaron opened a half-door leading to the back. "This is where the action happens. We keep all the dogs in crates until it's time to work on them."

Three large dogs whose breed she couldn't recall, and four small yippy creatures waited in the cages.

"Over on your left is the dryer cage. A small terrier growled inside. That's for the dogs who don't like the hand dryers or dogs that will need extra drying time before they're groomed. Sylvester there just hates everything about being groomed.

"Those hooks on the wall to your right are where we leash dogs that get anxious if left in crates. They do better if they can see the humans.

Notice the bigger run area behind you? It's for the larger dogs that wouldn't fit comfortably in the crates. Usually they aren't crated at home. They headed further into the room. Back here are the grooming tables. You'll meet Drew on Monday, he's another groomer. He's off today. Back here is our bathing room, and this is Lloyd, our groomer in training. He's a disabled veteran too."

Lloyd took a tiny terrier out of the tub and toweled it off as he offered Cassie a smile. "I'd shake your hand, but Puddin' here might bite you. She's not very social, and she hates being groomed." The tiny dog growled and bared her teeth. "Master Seargeant. Army."

"Captain. Airforce."

Lloyd grinned and wrapped the towel securely around the pooch, which seemed to calm the dog. "I assume if you're getting the tour, they hired you. Happy to have you onboard, Captain."

"How do you manage to bathe an aggressive dog, Sergeant?"

"Very carefully." Lloyd stroked the dog's head as he began growling again.

"What if he bites you?"

"It's part of the job." Aaron offered. "I've the scars to prove it."

Lloyd chuckled. "His backside has a nice scar from a scared rottweiler."

"Never turn your back on a female, they'll get you every time." Aaron laughed, leaving Cassie to wonder if there was a human female he was referring to.

"There's a dog run out this door behind the building. And this door to the left is our break room. Basically it's a large closet with a table. There are cubicles for backpacks and purses in there. You've seen our storage room slash office. That's it then."

"You'll begin training at the front desk starting Monday. I believe Marc will be showing you. My brother-in-law is a computer nerd. After he ran the front desk last year, he totally redid our computer system. If you're as good as your resume, you'll have no problem learning the system and running the front desk. Marc used to work in corporate America, so he had a lot of good ideas on how to make things better computer-wise. If he's not available Monday, Bria and I can get you started on the basics."

"I look forward to it." Cassie extended her left hand. A proper handshake involved the right, but she didn't want to risk squeezing too hard. His hand was larger, but his fingers the same length. She looked up at him, which was a rarity at her six-foot statue. A woman could get lost in those deep blue orbs. Shaking herself mentally, she nodded toward him.

"See you on Monday then."

She did a perfect military turn and strolled out the door, picking up her pace until she reached the corner. There was no way she was going to fantasize about a guy she'd scalded with coffee and who would be her boss. She pulled her keys from her slacks pocket and opened her 1969 mustang convertible. The midnight blue exterior contrasted with the red interior. Her late-brother had totally redone it before he passed. When he'd left it to her in his will, she almost refused. Traveling the world made it hard to maintain such a classic. Now she was happy to have it. Converting the transmission from stick to automatic had been worth the expense to have something of Ryan's to enjoy. She'd covered the white stirring wheel with a leather cover to keep it clean. The red interior was trimmed in white in honor of his military service. Ryan loved cars and flying. Cancer had taken him from the Air Force prematurely, just like her accident had.

She headed to her parents with a light heart. At last, this new chapter of her life could begin.

Chapter 2

Cassie dug through some boxes in her parents' spare room.

"What are you doing here?" Her mother asked. Alyson Quinn had the same auburn hair as her daughter, but that's where the resemblance stopped.

Her peachy complexion wasn't flooded with freckles. Something Cassie had been teased about her whole life. Dad's freckles and grandma's hazel eyes made her less attractive then her sister. She'd never cared about her looks before losing her arm. The loss made her feel ugly and the freckles just seemed to draw attention to it.

"Cassie, I ask what are you doing?"

Cassie pulled herself away from her musings. "I'm looking for work clothes." She took a blouse from the box and beamed at her mom. "I start my new job on Monday."

"Congratulations." Mom gave her a warm hug." Tell me about it."

"I'll be running the front office for Doggie Designer Duo." Cassie stiffened, expecting something negative about her new job. Mom was all about what others thought. Her position in the Air Force was something to brag about. A prosthetic arm was not. Now what would she say about a lowly job in a dog salon?

"Wonderful. I know Willis's." She beamed at her daughter. " The parents anyway Fine people. And Doggie Designer Duo has won a lot of awards. Well, at least that boy has." She sat beside Cassie and started sorting.

"His sister used to be a supermodel. But she gave that up. Can you imagine?" Her mother tssk. "But she seems happy as part owner of that place. She's also the president a Bow Wow Rescue. That woman loves dogs. She married a wonderful man last year." She raised her hand as if grasping for the information. "Marc Graham runs his marketing business from home. He lived with his grandmother Dolores Carter after his wife died. Tragic really. His son Tyler was in the car when his wife was killed."

Mother had a habit of spewing all the information she had on someone or something before she could settle to listen. Today Cassie didn't mind. The more she knew, the better able she would be to help her employers.

"What else do you know about Aaron?" She tried to sound casual.

Mom had found slacks and three pairs of jeans in another box and laid them beside the blouse on the bed. "Aaron Willis would give you the shirt off his back if you needed it." Her comment brought a picture of the shirt-less man to the forefront of her mind. Then she chuckled and related the coffee shop incident.

"I'm sure he doesn't hold that against you, dear." Mom smiled. "He was chubby kid. Then he joined football and worked out a lot. Your brother, Robert, sees him at the gym every day. And they're in that ridiculous Fantasy Football League. I don't understand that at all. I mean the football thing, not Aaron. He volunteers a lot. He lives on a farm with his folks and has three dogs. Wait." She put her hand up." He just moved to his sister's old home. When she married Marc, his grandmother gave them her home and moved into a senior living neighborhood. Two blocks over. Senior Oasis."

"Dare I ask how you know all this?"

"I attend church with them. And I've lived in this town since you joined the military, and Robert and Candace moved here." She laughed and gave her a side hug.

" Let's look over your wardrobe and see what you'll need. Then you're staying for dinner and sharing the good news with your father."

Cassie nodded. More of the heavy burden on her shoulder lightened, knowing that her mom didn't condemn her for her employment choice. Why should her approval matter after all these years?. She should just live her life the way she wanted and not worry about what her family thought. But old habits die hard. Her military job made her mother less prickly about her single state. Coming home with an arm missing seemed to soften her. The pity had slowly turned to acceptance. She was the only one unmarried of her siblings. Ryan's son was at the Air Force Academy. Robert and Candace had three darling girls under seven, and Carrie and Ricardo were too busy building their real estate business to have a family. The plus side of losing an arm was no more nagging about singleness.

Her heart ached at the prospect of never finding love, a husband, and children. She always thought there would be time. She'd date some in the military, but no one stirred her heart. Now the physical and emotional pain made her a bad candidate for marriage. And no one would ever convince her otherwise. Since the accident, no man had given her a second look. After discovering the prosthetic after their first look, they'd smiled and walked away. Tears formed in her eyes, she dashed them away.

Stiffening her back, she gathered the clothes they'd pulled out and headed to the laundry room.that would give her time to gather her thoughts before her dad came home. She could have done them in the laundry room at her apartment complex, but this would allow her time to relax when she got home. Focusing on her new job was far more productive them moping about what would never be.

COMING IN 2024!
Subscribe to Cindy's newsletter to stay up to date: https://bit.ly/ CindyErvinHuffNews

ALSO BY CINDY ERVIN HUFF

ABOUT THE AUTHOR

Cindy Ervin Huff is an Award-winning author of Historical and Contemporary Romance. She loves infusing hope into her stories of broken people. She's addicted to reading and chocolate. Her idea of a vacation is visiting historical sites and an ideal date with her hubby of almost fifty years would be the theater. Visit her website www.cindyervinhuff.com

Or on social media:

https://www.facebook.com/author.huff11
https://www.instagram.com/cindyervinhuff/
https://twitter.com/Cindyhuff11Huff
https://www.tiktok.com/@cindyehuff

Made in the USA
Monee, IL
03 November 2023

45736202R00111